TO THE ENDS OF THE EARTH

Skye Warren

Chapter One

I IMAGINE MY prince a hundred times a day. When I wake up on the dirt floor with the other girls, sunlight streaming through the painted-over window. When I clean and cook and perform my chores. Most of all I imagine him when it's time for afternoon prayers. That's when Leader Allen makes me confess my sins, whether I've done them or not.

Sarah Elizabeth, did you have impure thoughts?

That's when he punishes me.

My prince will have blond hair, even paler than mine. He'll have blue eyes that shine with goodness, with love. I want him to be almost pretty, his mouth in a bow and his eyelashes long. He'll be strong enough to slay my dragon, but he would never hurt me.

I'm sweeping the floor in Leader Allen's bedroom when I notice a cloud of dust through the window. That means someone is driving down the long lane separating Harmony Hills from the rest of the world. Maybe it's a delivery even though it's not Monday. Or maybe it's someone coming to visit Leader Allen. Even though he didn't have me prepare a special meal.

I drop my broom and cross the room to watch one, two, three huge black cars coming down the lane. Blood pumps through my veins. It's not a white steed, but it's close enough. My hands clench the windowsill hard enough for the old wood to creak.

Maybe God is finally answering my prayers.

My prince is here.

I don't feel the uneven floor on my bare feet as I fly down the stairs. Any other day I'd be worried about Leader Allen hearing me, worried about the punishment he'd give me for my lack of grace. Not today. It seems impossible, but I know it's true. He's here. I'm just minutes away from seeing his face for the first time.

A dark shadow looms on the other side of the door, tall and broad through the muted stained glass window. Every time Leader Allen preached about faith, *this* is what I believed in.

I reach for the knob, almost afraid to turn it. Afraid to find out I'm wrong.

And then what will I believe in?

My hand moves without my knowledge,

opening the door, letting light in. Except the man standing on the doorstep isn't my blond or blue eyed prince. He has dark hair and deep green eyes. And even though he looks strong enough to slay a dragon, to slay *twenty* dragons for sport, he doesn't look kind.

His hard gaze rakes over me, knowing and cruel.

The hope must still be burning in my eyes, leftover embers, because he gives a curt shake of his head, barely discernable, that steals my breath. No, he's not my prince.

A man this hard isn't anyone's prince.

Behind him I recognize the blonde curls of Sister Candace. Another man stands beside her, implacable and severe in a dark gray suit. Both men look terrifying, but Candace doesn't seem scared. She seems…proud. Strong. The way she holds her head high. I resented her for running away, for leaving me to serve in her place, but seeing her now, I can't resent her. If this is what she's like in the outside world, if this is how protected she is, she's better off gone.

The first man is solid and as thick as a tree trunk. From beneath the sleeves of his suit, tattoos snake over his skin. I imagine it circling him all the way around, vines that feed from him. In one hand he holds a black briefcase.

He shifts and I can see the leather beneath his jacket—a holster. For a gun. I know about guns even though I shouldn't.

I made myself learn, because I knew that my prince might never come.

One dark eyebrow lifts. *Let me in,* he says without words. *You don't want to find out what happens if you try to stop me.*

I don't want to stop him. If he's here to hurt Leader Allen, if he's here to help him—I won't stand in his way. But I'd almost rather he hurt me. Something physical to match the spiritual ache that's ripping me apart inside. I'm old enough to know that princes aren't real, that no one is coming for me. It was something I needed to believe. I still need to believe it, but in the face of this man's cold regard, I can't find any faith.

"This way," I whisper.

Footsteps follow behind me, none of them saying a word. I'm not really a person to them. I'm like the dirt road they drove on to get here. Something to use.

When we get to Leader Allen's study, I hover outside.

Only one time did I enter without knocking. Sister Jane collapsed in the kitchen, the heat sweltering with the ovens, her face cherry red. I ran straight into his study, stood in front of his desk, frantic as I told him what happened.

He got the bag of rice from one of his drawers and spread it on the floor. I knelt there for twenty minutes in punishment while he prayed for my soul. Sister Jane had to wait until we were through.

Both men go inside. They don't even knock.

Candace follows them, and the words stick in my throat. The warnings. *The rice.* I don't want it to happen to her. But I doubt it will happen, not with those two men. They might punish her themselves, but they won't let Leader Allen touch her.

I pretend to close the door, but I keep it open a crack. He'd make me kneel for an hour if he found me spying, but this feels too important. The man with the green eyes might not be my prince, but he might be my escape.

"I suppose you know who I am," one man says in a businesslike tone. "If Rosalie Toussaint's lawyer knew where to find her daughter, then you do too. And you know who she works for."

Leader Allen may know who they are, but I don't. The only thing I recognize is the name *Rosalie Toussaint.* That's Candace's mother. She had been in personal service to Leader Allen, which meant she attended his private prayer sessions. That's why everyone assumed Candace would follow suit, until she ran away.

And I was the one chosen to substitute.

True believers have to give all their worldly goods to the community. The fact that Rosalie Toussaint had a lawyer means she might have held something back.

Leader Allen's gravelly voice rings out. "I always knew you had the devil in you, girl."

He's talking to Candace. She's the one who tempts men to sin. She probably tempted the man in the dark gray suit to sin. That's why he came here on her behalf. Maybe there are benefits to sin. *Protection.*

The men drop their voices, and even with the crack in the door I can't make out their words. All I can hear is the menace between them, the threats in the air.

One of the men says, "Maybe you don't care about your own life, but I'm sure you care about your flock."

If I needed any assurance that these men aren't here to save me, this is it. We're not people to protect. Not women to sin with, like Candace. We're collateral.

Leader Allen laughs. "Take them then. Kill them. Fuck them."

I gasp, stepping back from the door. These men are here to hurt us.

And Leader Allen doesn't care.

Even while I hoped and wished for a prince, I knew he wasn't real. So I listened very carefully whenever the men discussed guns. I watched behind the wheat shed while they taught the boys to shoot.

And when no one was looking I hid a rifle away.

It only takes me a second to retrieve it from under the floorboard in the pantry. Then I'm back in front of the office, nudging the door open with the butt of the gun. It takes both my arms to hold it up, but my aim is steady. Right behind the desk.

I pull back the hammer.

Candace whirls to face me, her pretty blue eyes widening. "You don't want to do this," she says. "He's not your enemy."

Who does she mean, Leader Allen? Or the man with dark green eyes? Either way she's wrong. They're all my enemies. My prince isn't coming. I need to do this myself.

"I have to. This is my only chance. Move out

of the way."

I step sideways so I can hit Leader Allen without hurting anyone else. I take my aim—

"Sarah Elizabeth. Don't." Candace pushes the rifle toward the wall. Why does she want to protect him? Doesn't she know what he did to me?

My gaze meets hers, and I see the worry. She knows. And she's trying to—what? Protect me? To keep me from becoming a murderer? In a flash of morbid humor I realize that she might be my prince, after all. Kind and good. Blonde and beautiful.

"That's right, girl," Leader Allen says to Candace. "You wouldn't kill your father, would you?"

Her father? She looks as shocked as me. As sickened.

Leader Allen groomed her to take her mother's place—and all the while he knew he was her father? I'm not sure how it's possible, because Rosalie Toussaint already had a little girl when she came to live in Harmony Hills. Anything could have happened before that. And it doesn't really matter, because whether or not he's her father—he deserves to die. For hurting her.

For hurting *me*.

I raise the rifle, almost toppling over at its

weight. Then someone touches me—the man with green eyes. He puts his hand on my shoulder, turning me around. And every time I've ever been held down on the prayer mat, every time I've ever knelt on dry rice comes back to me. My finger closes on the trigger in dark reflex.

A loud *bang* rings through the air, along with the metallic tang of blood. Blood spreads over white fabric. Green eyes flash with pain, with shock. With vicious intent. What have I done? Distantly I hear three more gunshots. Not mine.

I look over to see the man in the silver suit holding a gun, expression grim and savagely satisfied. Leader Allen's bleeding body slumps to the ground.

He's dead.

The person who touched me. Who forced me. He'll never pray with me again. Never pray with anyone. And I know that despite every single one of his sermons that he isn't going to heaven. He doesn't deserve to.

The man with the green eyes turns to me. "Let's go, little bird."

My eyes widen. "What?"

"I'm not leaving you here," he snarls, looking as fierce as any demon. *Because I shot him.*

I hid that rifle under the floorboard six months ago, dreaming of the day when I'd use it.

And never daring to think about the blood that would follow. It spills across his chest, bright and crimson. I hadn't meant to hurt him, but he doesn't know that. He doesn't care. What will he do to me? Leader Allen was a man of God, and his punishment had been harsh. And this man, this man of tattoos and guns—his will be worse. "I'm sorry," I whisper.

He reaches for my wrist. A twist, and the rifle falls to the floor.

I only have a second to react before he hauls me into his arms. *He's taking me.* I don't know how he manages to pull me when he's been *shot,* but we're leaving the house at a rapid pace. No no no. I only got free from Leader Allen two seconds ago. I won't be held captive by yet another man with dark intentions. I'm punching him, yelling at him. Anything. Everything.

The sunlight blinds me, the world a blur of light spots and green eyes.

A shot rings out. Are they shooting someone else?

Dirt sprays against my leg, and I realize that someone is shooting at *us.* The men of Harmony Hills must have realized that their leader is dead. They're fighting back.

The man shoves me into one of the large black cars and climbs in after me.

I scramble back, trying to get out. If he closes that door, I'm trapped.

With a cruel wrench, he twists me into the seat. The door closes as loud as a gunshot. Tires squeal as they fight the dirt for purchase. The car moves forward fast enough to lock me into the seat.

"No," I'm shouting, crying. "Let me go."

What will he do to me? How will he punish me? I hated the prayer sessions, the dry rice beneath my knees, but at least I knew what to expect. This is my home.

"They'll kill you," he growls. "Don't you get that? You were in the room with us. You held a fucking gun on him. Doesn't matter if your bullet ended up inside me or him. They'll come for you. And no one here will protect you."

He may as well have shot me, instead of the other way around. There's a hole where all my fight had been, my struggle, spilling scarlet. "How do you know that?"

"Because if there was, you wouldn't have been in that house."

And I leave Harmony Hills, not on the back of a white horse, holding my prince.

I leave with the devil himself.

Chapter Two

His name is Luca.

I learn that early, from the driver of the big black car we're in. I can't see him through the dark-glass divider, but I hear him over some kind of speaker system. "Where to?"

"Away from this hellhole," he snarls. "I'll need to stop in a few hours. I'm hit."

A whistle. "Someone shot you? Damn, Luca, you're losing your touch."

Green eyes narrow on me. "Don't worry. I'll get mine."

My heart thuds against my ribs. What will he get? What will he do to me?

"Open that," he says softly, voice laced with menace.

I glance sideways at the glossy wooden panel. Is there a gun inside? He's waiting for me, infinite patience while blood continues to seep onto his white shirt. My hands grope at the smooth surface, searching for a latch. I must find it, because a small door levers open.

Inside a compartment there's a neat stash of alcohol swabs, of cotton gauze.

A first aid kit is more terrifying than a weapon. How violent is this man?

His voice runs over my skin, dark and silky. "You need to clean the blood first."

My breath catches. He takes off his shirt, revealing miles of muscle, tan skin, and tattoos up his arm. The wound looked extreme with blood spilling out, but it hardly registers against the hard-shaped masculinity of this man. He looks like he could have been shot four times and kept going, a machine built from sinew and stone.

He gestures to the cabinet. "Alcohol wipes."

I jump at the reminder, pulling out three packets with shaking hands.

His body reclines in the seat, watching me through hooded eyes. He wants me to clean the blood? It's fair, considering I'm the reason he's wounded. Except that will mean getting close to him. It will mean touching him.

The car sways gentle from the deeply rutted road. It will be an hour until we hit the farmer's market where I sometimes help sell vegetables. And beyond that? I don't know what's beyond these hills, but I'm about to find out.

Keep my back against the side of the car, I scoot around to his side. Already it feels warmer, this close to his body. Like he's vibrating with energy even while he stays still.

A single drop of blood works down his chest, drawing through the smear left by his shirt. It's a portrait of anger, of control. It's a portrait of the despair I felt in that moment.

I fumble with the heavy packets, producing a white cloth. The sharp tang of alcohol fills space. I wrap the damp fabric around my finger, forming a point. He's still too far to reach, so I scoot a little closer. We're not touching anywhere, but he's close enough to grab me.

There's a lump in my throat. Every time I've ever fought.

Every time I've ever *lost*.

It builds inside me until the same sense of despair overcomes me. My finger on the trigger. My heart in pieces. My alcohol-swab-covered finger against his tanned skin, white on dark with crimson soaking through.

"Are you afraid of me?" he asks, but he must know the answer.

"You're a sinner."

He laughs, the sound reaching into the shadows of my heart. "And what do you think your precious Leader Allen was? Was he a saint?"

I look away, unable to face the mocking in his eyes.

His thumb and forefinger captures my chin. He makes me confront him, his green eyes serious now. "What did he do to you, little bird?"

He punished me. "The same thing you're going to do."

He strokes my skin, almost absently, considering this. "Did he tie you up?"

My heart jumps. Leader Allen didn't need to restrain me. "No."

"Did he beat you?"

Sometimes, but mostly I knew better than to fight. "Are you going to beat me?"

A slow smile. "No, little bird. You're going to like what I do."

Because I'll have learned my lesson? "Please."

His eyes narrow. "You want mercy now? When I've got a fucking bullet in my shoulder because of you? I'm not a merciful man, little bird. A fighter. An enforcer. A fucking bulldozer. That's what I am."

I swallow hard before pulling out a fresh alcohol swab. This one I have to touch closer to the wound, on the burnt skin itself. "Not mercy for me."

He doesn't flinch. He doesn't even move. "For who? For whoever your precious leader sent to scare Candy at the club? Because that's the first question Ivan's going to ask you when we stop."

My heart squeezes. Candy—is that her name now? I knew her as Sister Candace. I clenched my fists every time Leader Allen talked about her, half-praying he'd never find her. Half-praying he *would* find her so that he'd leave me alone. And the worst part is he sent my brother. His best soldier.

When the wound is clean, I pull out clean gauze and tape.

It doesn't seem like enough for a bullet wound.

"Will this be…okay?"

"Don't worry," he says, sounding amused. "I won't die anytime soon. Not before I've had a chance to find out your secrets. Not before I pay you back."

I shudder, smoothing the tape over his skin. His muscles ripple under my touch.

And then I'm finished, except I don't move away. I set the bloodied wipes aside and kneel at his feet. We're in the car, but I have enough experience in this position to hold myself with grace. I have enough experience in this position to know what he'll want from me.

My hands are stained red from his blood, dark and dry. I move them to his pants, opening the clasp. His large hand covers both of mine, stilling me.

"What the fuck are you doing?" he demands.

I flinch at the word *fuck*. It's a plea. A prayer. I'll give him this in the hopes that he'll be soft with me. Because it isn't only me he'd hurt. Isn't only my brother. There's another life at stake. "I'm pregnant," I whisper.

I hadn't wanted to tell Leader Allen, but he noticed my lack of courses. He noticed the small bump during prayers. And he declared the baby a child of God.

Luca showed no pain during the entire time I cleaned his gunshot wound.

Now he sucks in a breath. "Whose child is it?"

I meet his emerald gaze, certain of this much. "Leader Allen."

Fury flashes across his face. "He forced you."

He didn't have to. There are no choices in Harmony Hills—not for women, not for children. Not for me. "I'm not sorry he's gone."

"No," he murmurs. "You were ready to shoot him. Instead you shot me, because you think I'm the same."

I see the way he looks at my body beneath the shift. I see the hard ridge in his pants when I'm near him. He wants the same thing that Leader Allen took from me. And maybe I could have survived that, if I didn't have someone else to think about.

We stop in a city so large it takes my breath away.

There's a hotel room with windows that look out over the buildings, so high it makes me dizzy. In that room Luca steals some of my secrets. He makes me tell him who Leader Allen sent. My brother. Alex. I don't know whether Alex deserves to be punished, to be killed, for what he's done, but I don't want to be the one to cause it. My only solace is that he never returned after his last mission. Luca will have to find him first.

It's a shock that Luca doesn't take my body, even though I see the way he looks at me. I feel the way he tightens whenever he touches me. It's only a matter of time.

Only a matter of time before I escape from him, too.

I have to, because I'll never trust a man again. I can't risk it, because more than anyone I know what they're capable of. And I have someone else to protect.

So I run from him. Candace helps me with that.

No matter how hard he tries, he'll never catch

me. I'll run until my legs give out, until my dying breath. There's a child inside me, one who deserves a life without violence. Without pain.

Maybe I deserved that too.

Chapter Three

One year later

THE NIGHT PASSES in a dark blur of grabbing hands and sloshing amber liquid. There are too many faces to remember, and why would I want to? They're either drunk out of their minds or leering at me. The tiny top I'm wearing with the Last Stop's compass logo emblazoned across my breasts doesn't help. Neither does the short skirt that's part of the uniform.

I'm lucky it covers the white fabric of my panties. When you need to get paid in cash, there aren't many options. I've worked in the steamy cavern of dry cleaners, looking the other way as drugs were sold out the back door. I've cleaned houses and barely escaped from one overzealous customer's bedroom. I can't say that I enjoy working at the beer-and-wings joint, but at least it's honest work that pays well.

At the end of the night I count my tips and come up with seventy-four dollars and a heavy handful of change. Enough to pay the sitter, get food for the week, and put some in my emergency fund.

Angelica grabs another stool beside me. I don't know much about her, but she works well and always has a smile for the customers. Now she looks tired, probably reflecting my own exhaustion. "Not bad," she says, nodding toward my small stack of cash.

"Thanks, but I'm guessing you have me beat." She was already here when I started working.

Every time I move, I end up a little farther from home. Texas, New Mexico. A detour over to Oregon and then straight north to Canada. Crossing the border was easy, but finding work without the proper work visas was harder outside the country. But I can't stop. That's how they catch me.

I kept moving north, crossing the Aleution Islands by ferry. That was two months ago, when the cold Alaskan summer felt comparable to a hill country freeze. I'm not sure what we'll do when the winter hits hard, but I've learned not to plan too far ahead.

Angelica shrugs. "I let them cop a feel. Not too many women around here. They're hard up. You could earn more if you wanted to."

They cop a feel whether I let them or not. "This is more than I made at my last job."

"You gonna tell me where that was?" When I don't answer, she gives me a slight smile. "Didn't think so."

I can't trust anyone, not even someone in the same position as me. I learned that a long time ago. People will betray you if they get the chance. They'll leave you if they can. And unlike before, I'm not only looking out for myself.

"Nothing personal," I say, slipping the cash into my little apron.

"A few of us are heading to Dominic's house. He usually has good shit."

That was probably slang for drugs or something. Weed? Coke? Maybe if I'd grown up in a regular house with regular friends, I'd know. "I can't."

I start to turn away, but she stops me with a softly spoken, "Beth."

The way she says it, it's almost a question. She knows it might not be my name. It's common enough that I usually use it. And that way I can answer to it when someone calls me. *Beth Smith. Beth Jones. Beth, Beth, Beth.*

Schooling my face into mild interest, I turn around.

Her eyes are narrow, studying my face. Memorizing it? Comparing it to a picture she's seen? My blood chills. That frantic beat kicks up in my heart, the one that tells me to run, to hide.

I take a step back.

Her eyes flicker away. "Someone was asking about you."

The knot in my stomach turns hard and thick. I won't be able to breathe again until I see Delilah, safe and asleep in my arms. I won't be able to breathe again until we're fifty miles away. Except the nights are freezing. What if my old car busts on top of a mountain?

"Elizabeth," she says, her eyes knowing. "Blonde hair. Said you owed him some money."

There are two men after me, but neither want my money. One wants to save my soul. The other wants to own my body. Either way there's only one thing left to do. Whenever they get too close, I run.

I force my voice to remain even, conveying none of my panic. "Must be the wrong girl."

"Yeah," she says, not believing me for a second. "That's what I told them."

Relief floods my mouth, metallic after the rush of fear. If someone's this close to me, they'll find me soon. But it's good to have a reprieve, even if only a few hours' head start. "Thank you."

She hesitates. "They offered me fifty bucks for information."

My hands tighten on my rolled-up apron. If I need to go on the run again, I need all the money I can get. Gas money, convenience store food. Deposit at another crappy apartment.

Still, she protected me. That counts for something, doesn't it? I don't know anymore what true friendship would be. Maybe I never did. All I can hope for is the fleeting kindness of strangers. My fingers numb, I fumble for fifty dollars.

The slap of the cash on the scarred table surface is the only sound in the bar. She watches me, her eyes dark and mysterious. Did she really tell them I wasn't here? Or maybe they're already at my apartment. People will lie if I let them. Didn't I learn that a long time ago?

Without another word, I'm gone.

Chapter Four

THINGS GO FROM bad to worse when I twist the key to my car. Nothing happens. The engine doesn't even turn over. I squeeze my hands on the old leather steering wheel like it can feel my tension.

"Come on," I whisper. "Don't bail on me now."

I got the car down in Wyoming for five hundred dollars flat. That included the stolen plates. It's done well for me, but I don't have the money to get it fixed. I can't afford to stick around, either.

Light flashes off metal from the truck parking lot, around the side of the Last Stop. Most of the diners who come through are truckers. Either that or they work in the logging station about a mile down the road. All of them look rough and dangerous. Maybe that was my mistake, ending up in a place without many women. I stand out even though I keep my head down.

I step out of the car and lift up the hood as if I know anything about cars. I could bake a pie or recite all twelve-thousand words in the Book of Job. That's the skill set you get growing up in Harmony Hills. The first time I tried to use a microwave, I started a fire because I'd put tin foil inside.

The crunch of boots on the brittle ground makes me stiffen.

"What's wrong, little girl?"

"Nothing."

There must be some kind of sixth sense men have when a woman is desperate. They come out of the woodwork like they were just waiting for the signal. Another man approaches us, his gait unsteady enough to tell me he's flat drunk. As he passes under the single parking lot lamp, I get a good look at his face. Jimmy John. Two names, just like that. He works at the logging station. The other man, I'm guessing he's got a rig.

I get enough crude offers every night bussing tables to know what either of these men would want in exchange for a ride to my apartment. It's easy to say no. I've had enough of men's desire to last a lifetime. Less easy to make sure they respect my answer.

"Looks to me like you've got yourself in a bit

of trouble," says Jimmy John.

"My boyfriend's on the way." This is one of the few times in my life I wish I had a man around. A man like Luca Almanzar, who could pound any one of these men into the pavement. And how long would it have taken for him to turn his fists on me?

The first man steps back. That's how things work around here. You don't touch a woman unless you want a fight with her man. A woman alone is fair game. There's a reason this place is called the Last Stop. We're far from civilization now.

Jimmy John smiles, his gold tooth glinting in the moonlight. "Now, darling. I've seen you in here every night for two months. You ain't never mentioned a boyfriend before. You wouldn't be lying to Jimmy John, now would you?"

My voice only shakes a little on the lie. "Fine, you go ahead and wait around. See what happens when he gets here. But he's got a temper. I should know."

His eyes narrow. "All right. I'll just be waiting over there. We'll see who shows up, then, won't we?"

Both men head over to the front of the building, gone dark now after 4 a.m. I don't know whether Angelica's inside, but if I looked for her, I'd prove there's no boyfriend. And then we'd both be in trouble. Besides, I'll have to pass them to get to the door.

Men with too much to drink, too much desire. I've learned not to provoke them.

I make a show of pulling out my phone, as if I'm checking for a call from my boyfriend. The truth is I ran out of minutes on my prepaid months ago. It hasn't been a priority, not with the high gas bill keeping the apartment warm.

My apartment is within walking distance. Maybe I'd make it there before they catch me.

Maybe not.

Cold air whistles through the seams in my jacket. I bought this at a thrift shop in Oregon. It can't do much against the frigid Alaska air. My options are running out fast, sand through my fingers. If these men don't get me, the cold will. And Delilah is back at the apartment building, maybe in danger. My daughter. My little girl.

When I was back in Harmony Hills, courage felt like an impossible mountain to climb. I'd never be strong enough to fight back against my mama or Leader Allen. I'd never be free.

Then I got pregnant. From the first time Delilah kicked inside me, courage came easy. I'd do anything for her. That's how I got the strength to steal the rifle. And it's how I get the strength to bolt from my car. My Mary Janes slap the gravel, breath coming in freezing bursts. The whole world seems to blur, as if I've fallen through cracked ice.

From far away I hear shouts, the sound of boots coming after me.

Please, God, I pray. *If there was ever a time I need to be delivered from evil…*

He never answered my prayers before. He doesn't do that now either.

A hand wraps in my long hair. I've never been able to cut it. There's so much I never got to do. Then I'm yanked back, legs scraping against sharp rocks, landing hard on my palms.

Jimmy John sneers down at me. He swings one leg over me, climbing on top right in the parking lot. They aren't just going to hurt me, I realize. They're going to kill me. If not from my injuries, then from exposure. I'm never leaving the Last Stop after tonight. More men surround me, some carrying bottles of liquor, shouting, cheering. There's no walking away from this.

An inhuman roar splits the night, and the hair on the back of my neck prickles. I see the whites of Jimmy John's eyes a second before he looks up.

Something slams into his face, and he topples backward. I don't wait to see who hit him or why.

All I can see are two men fighting, hulking shadows in the dark. The other men have backed up to give them space. One man pins the other to the concrete, his fists a steady rain. The one slumps, his open mouth revealing the glint of gold. Jimmy John. Is he unconscious? Dead?

The man who's beating him swings toward me.

Shock jolts through me. "Luca?"

"Get out of here," he growls.

His face is twisted in a snarl, the light in his green eyes almost otherworldly. It wasn't God who answered my call for help. It's the devil himself, come to bring me home.

I don't want to see who wins the fight. I run like the hounds of hell are at my feet.

It takes only minutes to run from the parking lot to the road, but it feels like eternity in these shoes. Loose change spills from my apron, but I don't have time to stop.

For a breathless moment I hear someone following me, footsteps pounding closer. I glance over my shoulder in time to see a man running after me. The report of the gun echoes through the cavernous landscape. The man falls to the ground, revealing Luca holding a gun. *He saved me.*

Our eyes lock. Time stills. There's only him and me in the endless frozen desert, the black hole on land. He found me here. He must have been the one asking questions about me.

A punch to his jaw breaks the connection. While he's down, they jump on him like a pack of hyenas, tearing at him from all sides. Luca is built for fighting, muscle packed on muscle, but he doesn't stand a chance.

They're going to kill him.

That's what they would have done to me. Every cell in my body wants to run back and help him. I know I'd die too, but some things are worth dying for. And that's why I have to leave. Delilah needs me.

"I'm sorry," I whisper before I turn and run.

Chapter Five

By the time I see my apartment over the hill, I've lost them.

There aren't any footsteps behind me. The men were too busy beating the life out of Luca to follow me. An image flashes through my mind—Luca's powerful body, the pack of men surrounding him. My stomach clenches, and I put my hands against it, doubling over.

The night air is thick in my throat, threatening to choke me. Tears prick my eyes, but I force them back. There's no time for weakness. No room for emotion in my life.

I climb the rickety metal steps that sway when you use them. The wind plays a haunting melody through the rusted rails, growing louder as the night gets cold.

A rustle of white ruffled lace.

Mrs. Lawson opens the door before I can knock. She listens for the telltale song of the stairs. "What a night," she says, shivering at the gust of outside air. "Come inside, child. Quick."

I step into the dimly lit room, looking at the comforting family pictures for the last time. Mrs. Lawson is a large black woman who gave birth to four sons. They're shown as babies, as children. As smirking teenage boys. A couple are wearing military uniforms. Then the pictures stop. I've never worked up the courage to ask what happened to them, and now I never will.

The heat in her apartment abrades my skin, a painful warmth. "Is she okay?"

"Of course, child. She went down easy tonight. You must have tired her out with all that story time. How many times did you have to read about that mouse?"

"I lost count after ten."

My feet are bringing me down the small hallway to the very end. The door is open, light off. Delilah's little fist is visible, having fallen outside the blanket. Her dark curls cover her expression, but I know she's sleeping. Lord knows she doesn't stay still that long if she isn't. Sometimes she struggles to fall asleep, but she always stays that way once she does. No amount of sound can wake her.

"What's wrong?" Mrs. Lawson asks softly, standing beside me.

"I've got to go." My throat clenches because we had a good thing going. Delilah's sweet on Mrs. Lawson and her many pictures. That girl loves stories. "I can pay you through the end of the week, but—"

"No, child. If it's as bad as I think, then you're going to need it more than me."

I need so much more than I have saved, especially with my car broken and stuck at the Last Stop. The men probably took a bat to it once they finished with Luca. My heart squeezes. Why did he come after me? Why did he protect me? Except I know the answer to that.

He wants the same thing Leader Allen took— my body.

The fact that I don't have a car means I need a plan. I can't hitch a ride with a baby in tow, especially not in freezing weather. A cab is probably the fastest way to get out of here. Easy to track, especially with so few people around, so I won't be able to rest.

Maybe I'll catch a bus to Anchorage. And from there, who knows?

"I've got to pack," I say, taking one more fortifying glance at the dark curls I love. "Can you watch her for a few minutes? I'll be back in under an hour to get her."

"Of course," Mrs. Lawson says, her eyes serious. Whatever she's been through in life, she understands hardship. She understands fear.

My daughter is the only good thing to come of the sixteen years I spent in Harmony Hills. The hard prayer floors, the painful nights spent in divine worship. That's what Leader Allen called it when he made me kneel, when he forced my legs apart.

For years I sinned in my sleep, dreaming of killing him. Rescue came in the strangest form, maybe the only place it could have—from a man far more dangerous.

From Luca Almanzar.

An enforcer for organized crime, Luca's done unspeakable things. He did some of them to me—taking me captive, tying me up, keeping me in his hotel bed. Something strange happened to my body when I saw him, a heat that I didn't know how to name.

That doesn't matter now. He's gone. Only Delilah matters.

Chapter Six

I PACK THE paisley suitcase we have from Goodwill with its fraying threads and broken zipper. There's more than usual because of the bulky jackets we had to get, so I pack the rest in a white trash bag. The crackers and cereal from the pantry come with us. The stuff in the fridge will have to stay here. Only fifteen minutes until the cab's supposed to arrive.

There's one thing left in the apartment that's mine.

I keep it under the sink in the bathroom, next to a stained bucket that was here when we moved in. It feels like the place farthest away from us, as if I'm storing a ticking time bomb. This book is the only trace of my past. The only proof of what really happened.

It's hard to pick it up but harder to leave it. That's why I've dragged it around every place we've gone—a millstone. A burden. I stand, muscles protesting after a long day and a desperate run. The Bible feels like it weighs a thousand pounds.

The lights in the bathroom go out.

In the whole apartment.

A storm. It happens often enough up here, taking the whole power grid down. Except the heavy light from outside the apartment is still on, casting a faint glow through the window.

"Thought you could get away from me?" comes a low masculine voice.

Oh God. Not a storm. It's Luca. Somehow he got away from those men. Somehow he followed me. I whirl, holding the Bible against my chest. I hate having it this close. It's more than a bomb. It's radioactive, toxic to anything nearby. But I can't let him have it.

He's only a shadow in the dark, his large frame filling the doorway.

"What are you doing here?" I manage, my voice wavery.

He laughs. "Little bird, you know why I'm here."

"Because you want me." He took me to save me. That's what he said. His body betrayed the real reason. The same reason Leader Allen prayed with me.

"That's only the beginning," he says, his voice

low with promise. "I've been chasing you a long time. You've got a lot to answer for."

I take a step back. "Please let me go."

"Where do you want to go?" he asks, his voice mocking. "Farther north to Denmark? To Iceland? Or maybe all the way to the Arctic."

My heart sinks because there's nowhere left to go. Wherever I run, he'll find me.

Which means that Alex can find me too. Luca only cares about my body. He wants to do things to me, to sin with me. He wants divine worship with me. I've survived it before. I would survive it again. But if he can find me, that means Alex won't be far behind. And what he wants is much worse. My brother wants to return me to Harmony Hills. And he wants my daughter most of all.

"Fine," I say, my voice breaking. I toss the Bible onto the back of the toilet and reach for the hem of my shirt. I didn't waste time changing, so I'm still wearing the Last Stop's uniform. It comes off easy, leaving only a plain white bra underneath.

He sucks in a breath. "What the fuck are you doing?"

"I'm going to f-f-fuck you. Then you can leave." That's the thing about courage; it's a double-edged sword. It smooths the way toward doing things you never dreamed. I'll do anything to convince him to leave us alone. I will do anything to keep my daughter safe.

His growl makes the hair on my neck stand up.

"You're not going anywhere." He flicks the bathroom light on, revealing the gruesome spray of blood across his face. I cry out at the gash over his eye, the long ridge of dried blood along his chest. He looks like a gladiator after a long-drawn-out battle in the arena.

And he didn't just manage to escape. He must have killed those men. That's the only way he could have managed to leave that parking lot. All those lives on my head.

More pain. More death. No matter how fast I run, I can't seem to escape it.

"I don't understand," I whisper. "Why me?"

In the world he comes from there are a hundred beautiful women. Women who know how to wear pretty dresses and put on makeup. Women who know how to please a man as intense as Luca. Candace used to live in Harmony Hills with me. She was the first person to ever get out alive. And she turned herself into a siren, someone who could command men with a single flick of her perfectly manicured nail. She did it to prove that she could. And I...well, I can't. I haven't even been able to cut my long hair.

He steps close, and I'm suddenly more aware of my naked tummy, my breasts covered only by a single layer of fabric. My chest rises and falls with heavy, panicked breaths.

"You captured me, little bird." He trails a blunt finger down my temple, lifting a long blonde lock. It looks pale and silky against his scarred fingertip. "I follow you for the same reason you run."

I run because I'm afraid, but Luca isn't afraid of anything.

I run because I love my daughter, but a man as hardened as Luca doesn't know how to love. Most of all I run because my brother, Alex, chases me.

Leader Allen convinced him my daughter is the result of immaculate conception. He believes that Leader Allen never touched me in those prayer sessions. And as the holy daughter of Harmony Hills, he's bound to bring her back to the flock—whatever's left of it after Leader Allen died. There are bigger forces that move us, a larger hand that guides our way.

"I'll give you anything you want, if only—"

"If only I let you keep running? If only I

watch you fall right into the trap your psycho brother's set? If only I pretend I don't give a shit what happens to you? No, Sarah Elizabeth."

"Beth," I whisper.

My name in Harmony Hills was Sarah Elizabeth. Beth's the name I chose for myself.

"Beth," he says, voice rich with possession. "I'm going to keep you safe."

I don't care what happens to me. "My daughter."

"Don't you think I can protect her? I have resources, little bird."

He has cages. I'm not sure how safe he'll keep my daughter or the price we'd have to pay. I don't know how she'll grow up in a city as sinful as Tanglewood. I haven't been able to shed my restrictions like Candace.

I'm not comfortable with drugs, with violence.

With sex.

"What are you afraid of?" he asks, low and seductive.

The answer comes from somewhere deep inside me. "That I'll like it."

And then where would Delilah be? I know that what Leader Allen did to me wasn't right, but that doesn't mean everything he preached was wrong. I can't be the woman who likes those things, who cuts her hair. I want Delilah to have a choice about who she'll be. That can't happen with my brother and his extreme allegiance to Leader Allen's teachings. It can't happen in Tanglewood either, mired in the mafia, next door to a strip club.

I want her to have a fighting chance.

"Let's make a deal," he says, voice mesmerizing.

My stomach twists because that feels like a trap. I'm a starving mouse looking at the shiny metal springs, wondering if I can beat them. Wondering if it's still worth it if I can't. "What kind of deal?"

"Work with me to make sure Delilah is safe. Then you can decide where to go. Anywhere in the whole fucking world. I'll take you there myself."

"And leave me there?" I ask, holding my breath. Would he let me go?

He hesitates only a minute. "You can stay."

Chapter Seven

While I'm thinking of my answer, debating whether I can trust him, he plucks the Bible from the back of the toilet. As casual as can be, he strolls toward the light off the kitchen. The heavy book flips open. I manage to grab my shirt, pulling it on as I run after him.

I'm two steps behind him, reaching for the book. What page does he see?

"'In the beginning God created the heavens and the earth,'" he says. "'The earth was formless and void.'"

"'And darkness was over the surface of the deep,'" I whisper. Genesis.

He looks at me sideways. "Do you have the whole thing memorized?"

Shame clenches my throat. "That was the only way I could know it. I didn't know how to read."

Candace taught me a little bit when she helped me escape Luca. Then she went back to Ivan Tabakov, a man renowned for his cruelty.

Now she's called Candy, because she's a different girl. A smart, sexy, strong person. Not like me.

And I had to keep running. Had to give my child some chance at a normal life, the kind without cults, without criminals. There are people who live that way. I pass them, their windows dark as they sleep, but I can't seem to *become* them.

His hand touches mine, his fingers large and calloused against the back of my hand. "Beth."

I blink away the dark memories. "Why would you help me?"

"I'm a selfish man," he says. "I want you. I've wanted you from the moment I saw you in that godforsaken house, wearing that see-through shift and holding a rifle."

"Then why?" I gesture helplessly to the bathroom, where he'd turned me down.

His hand curls along the side of my arm, tickling me. I twist away from the sensation, and he uses the motion to hold my hand. Skin to skin. Palm to palm. His thumb sweeps over the tender skin. This shouldn't feel so intimate—soul to soul.

His green eyes glitter. "When I fuck you, you're going to want it. Understand?"

I swallow hard. "I don't—"

"No, you don't understand. Which is a damn shame considering you gave birth to a child. But I'm going to fucking teach you if it kills me."

The memory comes to me, that strange heat in my body. The laxness of my limbs. Is that what he means? Is this what it means to sin? My thoughts swerve away because I have my hands full with survival.

"You said you could make Delilah safe?"

His eyes narrow, but he lets me change the subject. It's the only subject that matters. "Yes, but the first thing we need to do is get her out of this godforsaken state. When God made the surface of the deep, I'm pretty sure he was talking about Alaska."

It's the worst thing I could do at a time like this, but somehow I find myself laughing. His irreverence, his insistence. The irrepressible feeling of safety I have whenever he's around. "Where will we go?"

"First we'll take Delilah down to Candy and Ivan. They'll watch her, keep her safe."

"No." Every cell of my body fights the idea of bringing Delilah into that nest of sin. Ivan Tabakov runs a criminal organization. He once owned the strip club where Candy worked when she escaped. That's not a place to raise a little girl.

That's not what normal is about.

"No one can get through Ivan's fortress of a house. Not even your brother."

Leader Allen sent my brother to terrorize the girls who worked for Ivan, threatening Candy so she'd come back to Harmony Hills. That plan backfired because Ivan had already fallen in love with her. His protection was fierce and brutal—resulting in Leader Allen's death. If anyone can protect Delilah, it's Ivan Tabakov. "We can't stay there forever."

"Not forever. Only until your brother is caught."

If my brother is caught, he'll be put on trial. He'll be found guilty. He's hurt people in the name of God. I know he deserves to be punished, but I'm still the product of my upbringing. I don't want to be the one to do it.

Delilah's little fist. Her dark curls. I'll do anything to protect her. And my brother won't rest until he finds me. Until he brings her back into the fold, the lost lamb.

Then I understand why Luca's really here. "You want to use me as bait."

It's a relief, after thinking he would force me. I shouldn't feel even the smallest pang of disappointment.

His jaw tightens. "Your brother went after the girls at the club. He went after Candy. Tabakov won't rest until he's been found."

"I'll do it," I whisper.

"I won't let you get hurt," he says, his voice hard.

He can't promise that, but it doesn't matter. It doesn't matter what happens to me.

Darkness was over the surface of the deep. The deep isn't really Alaska. It comes from the Hebrew word for chaos, for confusion. For the restless motion of waves. If there's one thing you learn from the Bible, it's metaphor.

The chaos continues until God creates the earth. The story is meant to tell us God's power, his might, but all I ever thought, as a little girl in a dirt-floor room, is that something existed before him.

The darkness was here first.

Chapter Eight

THAT'S HOW I end up at Mrs. Lawson's door again empty-handed. Luca stands a few yards back, watching to make sure no one from the Last Stop comes around. It makes me shiver to imagine those bodies—how many were there? They'll be hard by now, lying on the pavement. When will someone find them? It might not be until tomorrow at ten when the cook opens for lunch.

There's a move in the white lace. I'm sure Mrs. Lawson sees Luca. There's a longer pause before she opens the door. Her eyes narrow as she glances over my shoulder.

Luca normally looks terrifying, but with those bruises, the blood, it's an especially scary sight.

"It's okay, Mrs. Lawson."

Her harrumph says she knows what she knows. "Come inside, child."

As soon as she shuts the door, she turns the deadbolt. "I'm calling the police. Don't matter what he takes from your place or if he trashes it.

You and the child are both inside here, and he's not coming inside. Not without meeting the side of my baseball bat."

I give her a kiss on the cheek, and she blinks in surprise.

She'll be one of the few things I'll miss about Alaska. "He's not going to hurt me."

He's not going to hurt Delilah, which is the important thing. What he does to me alone, in the dark, when I'm his bait…that might hurt. Not the kind of pain he has now, from being hit and kicked. The kind inside you, in places you don't know about until they're rubbed raw.

The hallway is still dark, the door still open.

Delilah's still asleep, her dark curls stark against her curved cheek.

I pull her warm body into my arms, cuddling her close. She makes a sound almost like a squeak before nuzzling her face against me. She wears the warmest wool nightgown I could find in preparation for these little walks, her hands and feet covered with the same thick material. It helps even inside the apartments, where cracks in the insulation make it impossible to keep warm.

Mrs. Lawson blocks the doorway. "I'm not gonna see you again, am I?"

I can't ever come back here, even if I escape

Luca again. "I'll miss you."

She shakes her head. "If you ever need to run away from that man outside, you call me first."

My tears prick. When I imagined running all those years in Harmony Hills, I never thought anyone would help me. They told me stories about the sin outside. That didn't scare me half as much as the calloused disregard. We were a community, they said. We took care of our own.

They didn't take care of me, though. They hurt me. And I've found little pockets of community all along the way, shining like diamonds in the gutter.

"Thank you," I say, my voice thick.

She steps aside. "I'll miss that little angel, besides."

The little angel doesn't stir even when the cold night air touches her cheek. I say goodbye to Mrs. Lawson not with a word, but with a long look that tells a thousand warnings—the kind that women who've known violent men can share.

Luca's face looks worse under the flickering lamplight, more wild. He gazes down at Delilah's sleeping face with an expression I can't read. "We'll stay the night," he says. "Our flight leaves in the morning."

I don't know whether Delilah's sleeping face

gives us the reprieve, but I take it. Keeping her warm inside my apartment is hard enough. Out here it's below freezing.

"Thank you." I cross the small walkway quickly, slipping into my apartment with practiced ease. Luca follows behind, glancing around before locking us in.

Her little bedroll is still laid out in the one bedroom of the apartment, where she usually sleeps. She curls up against the pink and purple stars on the pillow, arms immediately wrapping around her stuffed unicorn. In some ways she'd had to live like me—in a bare room, with only a thin comforter as her mattress. In other ways her life is completely different, filled with color, with wonder. With love.

I turn to leave her and almost run into Luca.

"Dark hair," he says, but he's not looking at Delilah.

He's looking at my long blonde locks.

Delilah's curls crown her face, a beautiful raven color that I've never seen before. Leader Allen had already grayed by the time I knew him. I like to think it's hers alone, that she didn't even have a father. That's what my brother believes. That it was a virgin birth, the baby given to me by God. Only despite what I'd rather believe, I know the truth.

"It's beautiful," I say. "She's beautiful."

He nods. "Did you love him?"

I feared Leader Allen. I despised him. In a sick way maybe there was love too, in the form of necessity. The way you love air, unthinking, because you need it to live. I didn't fight him when he taught me the divine worship he wanted. Because I had no choice? Or because I was brainwashed? It doesn't matter. "I don't regret what happened. It gave me her."

He leaves the room, and I follow, shutting the door carefully so we don't disturb her. I'm already schooling my mind to accept whatever happens next. Whatever form of payment Luca desires. It's not so very different from Leader Allen. I need Luca to survive just as much.

In the luggage I find the white plastic box with FIRST AID written on it. "Let me take care of those cuts for you."

He gives me a strange look. "They don't hurt."

That seems impossible, but then maybe a man as tough as him doesn't feel pain like regular people. "It'll get infected."

After a hesitation he nods. I find a swab of alcohol and tear it from the packet. He stiffens when I approach, and I freeze. It's like walking up to a dog who's already bitten, who'll do it again. But he doesn't resist when I step close.

My hand reaches up to his neck.

He lowers his head.

The alcohol must sting against the open wounds, but I'm the one who sucks in a breath. Remembered pain. His blood drenches the little square cloth quickly. I work through two more packets before I'm done. He must bleed every time he fights.

"Who does this for you at home? When you fight in the ring?"

His voice has gone low and rough. "No one."

This close I can feel his breaths against my temple, his heat warming my front. The apartment isn't that much warmer than out there, especially outside the bedroom, but he feels like a furnace. When I turn away, my breast brushes against his arm. Embarrassment heats my cheeks as I find some antibacterial cream.

He stood still for the sting of the alcohol, but he pulls back from the soothing cream. It surprises me more than him when I give him a stern look. "Hold still."

His lip curls up in amusement. "Yes, ma'am."

I use a cotton swab to dab the cream on his

cuts. "Thank you."

He looks at me through slitted eyes, almost slumberous. "Why are you thanking me?"

"You saved me."

He makes a coarse sound. "You really have no idea, do you?"

I turn away, fussing with the little tube of cream. "What?"

"How many men I'd kill for you."

My eyes go wide. It's a horrible measurement, the number of deaths that would be on his hands, the amount of violence he'd commit. And yet it's a strange comfort too, knowing he would do that for me.

I throw away the bloody pieces and pack up the first-aid kit, using the excuse not to meet his eyes. "When will we go?"

"Tomorrow. Well, today. When you've had a chance to rest. I'll come to the door at noon."

Then I have to look at him. "Where will you go until then?"

"I'll sleep in my car."

"It's freezing out there!"

"That's where I slept last night."

I try not to think about him outside my apartment while I didn't know. How long has he been in Alaska, waiting for me, watching? And why does the thought make me feel safe instead of scared? "You can stay here."

His eyes narrow. "With you?"

"I mean it's nothing comfortable. Just the floor. But there's a blanket. And basic heating."

I'm not offering a blanket or heating. His car would probably be more comfortable on both counts. I'm offering my body. Maybe I should fight him, but I'm about to put the life of myself and my daughter into his hands. I want him to be as sympathetic to us as possible.

He studies me. Does he see my fear? My desire to please him? My mind is a mass of scripture notes. Already I'm trying to think of what he'd want. It was one thing when I planned to run away. Now that I'm hitching our fates to his, it's in my best interest to make him happy.

I dig out the blanket I sleep on, which was rolled up for travel, from my suitcase. Only when I throw it out over the carpet do I realize how pathetic it looks. Sleeping on the floor seems strange to most people, but it's all I've ever done. The few times we stopped at a motel, I could never get comfortable on a bed. I ended up on the floor by the end of the night.

"I hope this is okay," I whisper, flushed.

His gaze roams past the sad makeshift bed to

the corner, where the carpet curls up. To the ceiling, where leaks have turned the white plaster black. "It's not okay," he says gruffly.

My hands clench together. "I know Delilah deserves better."

His eyes narrow. "And you."

I'm not sure what I deserve, but it can't be good. By the rules of Harmony Hills I'd go to hell for leaving, for working in a bar. And of course for helping them fight Leader Allen. And by the rules of this society, what little I've been able to quilt together from scraps of conversations, what Leader Allen did to me makes me a freak. I don't belong anywhere.

All I can manage is a shrug.

He gestures to the bed. "What do you think is going to happen tonight?"

That's a loaded question. I don't want to whisper my fears aloud. I'm afraid I might be right. "Whatever you want?"

My voice curls up at the end, turning it into a question.

He grunts. "Get underneath the blanket."

This part I'm used to. It wasn't so cold in Harmony Hills, but I know how to lie on my back, how to squeeze my eyes shut. I know how to stay completely silent no matter what he does.

There's a soft rush of air as he lowers himself next to me. I feel his size like a looming shadow in the room, as large as a mountain. I'm a trickling valley stream, about to be crushed. Except he doesn't lay his body over mine. He lies next to me. He pulls me close, until I'm half on top of his body, my head pillowed by his chest.

"Sleep," he says.

My ear rests right by his heart. I can hear the steady *thump thump*. In contrast my heart beat's a mile a minute. My eyes are wide open, looking at the plain white apartment wall. A wall I've seen a thousand times but never like this. Never cradled in the arms of a man who could crush me.

I've slept with a man before. The proof of that is in the bedroom.

But I've never *slept* with a man before.

I bite my lip. "How—"

"Go to sleep, little bird."

It's impossible. He smells like the outside, like ice and pine—with a metallic undercurrent that I think might be blood. His chest moves steadily with his breath. It's like resting my head on the ocean.

And I never sleep well. It's not the carpet that bothers me. It's softer than the whitewashed wood slats in Harmony Hills. The memories haunt me most at night, when my hands aren't busy, when my mind is still. That's when I remember what Leader Allen did to me when everyone thought we were praying.

Luca's hand moves over my hair, brushing softly, petting. The rhythm combines with the motion of his body, lulling me into a kind of trance. His muscles are brick hard. They shouldn't be comfortable at all, but he's hot. Burning. A rare comfort in a cold frontier.

I press my face into him, my very own pink and purple pillow. My stuffed unicorn in the form of a hard-muscled man. My hand clenches a fistful of T-shirt, holding him there.

"Shh," he murmurs. "I'm watching over you. I'll keep you safe."

That's the last thing I hear before the night falls away, replaced only with deep, dark waters. They swirl around me in an endless tide, back and forth, dreamless and warm.

Chapter Nine

Most mornings when I wake up, Delilah is still asleep. Even with the sunlight coming in through the blinds, that girl can sleep. I can't complain because she's all smiles when she's awake.

If I've had a particularly rough night at the Last Stop, I might sleep in, which means I wake up to a snuggly body on top of me, chubby fingers grasping my hair.

This morning I wake up to the distant sounds of cheerful babbling.

A low voice responds, maybe asking a question.

More babbling, this time with a happy squeal as punctuation.

Rubbing the sleep from my eyes, I follow the sounds into the kitchen. What I find makes me blink, more confused than ever. There's a picnic happening on the cracked caramel linoleum, a thin blanket spread out. Luca sits across from

Delilah, him cross-legged, her little legs in front of her. Between them is a sleeve of crackers, an open jar of peanut butter, and a sippy cup.

"Do you want another one?" Luca asks.

Delilah responds with a string of syllables that probably mean *yes*, along with several other thoughts. She claps to illustrate her point. Or maybe to get him to hurry.

He doesn't hurry. He takes his time with a butter knife in the jar, spreading thick, creamy peanut butter onto the cracker, making it completely even. "Take a drink," he says, holding it out.

Her black curls shimmer under the kitchen light as she shakes her head. "No."

That's one of the few words she knows. And though I've never seen a more cheerful child, she also has a stubborn streak. She will say no plenty of times throughout the day, albeit cheerfully.

"One little sip."

Another string of baby talk, ending with a very clear, "Water."

"Water isn't my favorite either," he says reasonably. "But it's all I could find right now. Maybe they'll have milk on the plane."

With a sigh Delilah picks up the sippy cup for a brief sip.

Luca hands over the cracker, and she munches away. My heart has turned into something less muscle, more balloon—expanding, stretching beyond what I'd known I was capable of.

Seeing such a large, brutal man, his bruises even more prominent the morning after, at ease with my one-year-old daughter does strange things to my insides. There's guilt that she's had to grow up without a father. There's fear that this precious light will somehow be extinguished.

And worst of all, something like hope aches in my chest. Because Luca is so unbearably gentle in this moment. I hadn't known he could be like that. Hadn't dared imagine it.

As if sensing me, Luca looks up and meets my gaze. "Good morning."

The words catch in my throat. All I can do is nod.

He gestures to Delilah. "I hope this is okay. I didn't want to wake you."

"It's perfect," I whisper.

Carefully, so as not to disturb the picnic blanket, Luca stands. His body unfolds larger than I remembered, as if he's built for different rooms. Barracks instead of a crappy apartment. A gladiator ring instead of the parking lot of the Last Stop. He's a soldier. A fighter.

"The car's waiting outside," he says more quietly, glancing back at Delilah to make sure she's still occupied. She's given up on the cracker and is sticking her fingers directly in the jar.

"I'll just be a minute to pack what's left. You should have woken me up."

He frowns. "You didn't get enough sleep as it is."

My body agrees with him, reminding me that I had a long shift last night, the small aches and subtle bruises pointing out the places where Jimmy John grabbed me before Luca stepped in. "I'm fine," I say. "Whatever we need to do to get Delilah to safety."

His eyes narrow. "You'll be able to sleep on the plane."

"It doesn't matter."

The sound he makes raises the hair on my neck. "Someone needs to take care of you, little bird. If you aren't going to do it, then I sure as hell will."

I flinch. "Don't swear in front of her. Please."

"She doesn't mind."

My cheeks flush with warmth, a mixture of anger and embarrassment. I know that people swear out in the world. Adults use words like *hell* and *damn*. It doesn't mean anything. But I can't shake the twinge of fear I feel every time I hear them any more than I can cut my hair. I'm too well trained. I'm Leader Allen's creature, even now that he's dead.

Luca's expression softens. "I'll try not to swear."

I expected him to fight me to the death on this. How does a man like him take orders from someone like me? It doesn't make sense. He could have insulted me, called me names. He could have sworn a blue streak, and as long as he held the key to Delilah's safety, I would've had to bear it.

Instead he's given in, leaving me disarmed and off balance. "Thank you."

"I followed you from city to city, tracking you until I found you in that stink hole they call the Last Stop. How the hell—" He shakes his head, looking bewildered. "How did you survive in a place like that?"

Every word feels like a blow. Every touch I couldn't control rips at my soul. It was the hardest thing I ever had to do—and the easiest. I glance at Delilah, who has now turned the peanut butter jar upside down and created a cracker tower on top. "She makes everything possible."

He glances back at her. "Yeah. I think I'm starting to understand that."

I can't help but ask. "How did you track me?"

"That long hair," he says, laughing softly. "Bread crumbs wherever you go."

I manage not to flinch, but it still feels like a slap. It's a weakness, this hair. It's a weakness that I still feel beholden to all the tenets I was taught as a child. They were drilled into me. Literally written into my skin. I can't forget them any more than I can become a different person.

"Will you cut it?"

"Of course not," he says softly. "It's beautiful."

Awareness sinks in. "And it's part of the trap. The bread crumbs."

His eyes darken as he studies me. "Everywhere I went, people remembered your hair. That was the first thing, what people notice the first time they meet you."

"I'm not very good at hiding," I whisper.

"And then they all noticed something else. The way you brought soup to the elderly woman next door even though you're a single mother, with barely enough money to survive. How you fed the cats in the neighborhood until there was a damned—" He shakes his head, an abbreviated apology for swearing. "There was a buffet outside your back door. How you are always the first to give and the last person to take. Yes, you were the worst fucking—the worst at hiding, because you never stop helping. Even after what that monster did to you, you never stopped caring."

Chapter Ten

I TAKE REFUGE in the ordinary tasks I need to do—rolling up Delilah's sleep things and then mine. Washing the peanut butter off her face and brushing her two teeth. It's easier to focus on ordinary tasks than to think about what Luca said to me.

But his words are like a seed, and every moment that passes, it burrows a little deeper into the soil of my soul. There was water all along, a strange hope, a wistfulness that I could be something more than Sarah Elizabeth. That's why I called myself Beth when I left Harmony Hills, but that's just a name. Not a person.

I might be stronger than I thought. Might be memorable for more than just my long hair. At least Luca seems to think so—which is the most compelling realization of all. He sees me as more than my body.

Trucks are common in Alaska, with snow tires at this time of year. That's what I'm expecting when I go outside. Instead I find a string of three sleek black SUVs, a man in a suit standing beside one of them. These aren't limousines; these are their tougher, more protective cousins.

Inside the seats are covered in butter-soft beige leather, wood enamel along the door.

The pink car seat from my car, the one I left at the Last Stop, now sits in the middle of a wide back seat. Delilah clambers into her spot with relative ease, as if we normally use a car with low ambient lighting and a minifridge.

I buckle her in, feeling a little dazed. I think Luca might take one of the other SUVs—why do we need three of them? But he steps into the car after me, shutting us inside.

Absently I dig in my bag for a set of plastic rings, which Delilah prefers for car rides. She begins to teethe on them immediately, making delicate baby grunting sounds.

Luca sits in the forward seats, facing me, his expression enigmatic.

"Where did these come from?" I finally ask, unable to stop myself.

"After what happened last night, I called in reinforcements. I couldn't be sure whether those fuckers—those men would have relatives wanting revenge. I made sure we were covered for the ride to the airport."

I can't imagine the expense involved in getting these armed men, these glossy SUVs, out into the middle of nowhere. The newest car I've seen in weeks is a decade old, its back bumper torn off. This is a hard-scrabble place, which is a backward solace for me.

It's always reminded me of home.

The relief I feel at being safe is greater, though. I can't know what will happen next. Being bait for a man who's been indoctrinated by a murderer and abuser is hardly a safe destination. But as long as Delilah is alive, I don't care what happens to me.

Someone needs to take care of you, little bird. If you aren't going to do it, then I sure as hell will.

Luca's words come back to me in a rush of illicit pleasure. I can't deny that I like the idea of him taking care of me. Isn't that what he's doing? Even though he scares me, he's helping me protect Delilah. And he's using me to complete his orders from Ivan Tabakov. It's not a purely altruistic goal, nothing so special as love, but it's something. More than I've had before.

He remains quiet on the drive to the airport, only occasionally taking a phone call. From his terse replies, he's still coordinating our trip to

Tanglewood.

"Is the plane ready?" he asks.

Someone answers on the other end, sounding brusque.

"I don't fucking—I don't care," he says. "We're taking off in an hour either way, and your other client can go and… Well, they can just deal with it."

I have to smile at him, my throat a little tight, eyes too watery to be normal. It's the same way I felt watching him at the kitchen-floor picnic, this fighter turned soft by one sweet little girl.

Then his earlier words register. *The plane.*

My stomach drops. "Luca. I don't have a passport."

I don't have any form of identification at all. No driver's license. No birth certificate. According to the US government, I don't even exist. Harmony Hills didn't exactly follow legal procedures when babies were born. The less interference from the government the better.

Actually Delilah doesn't exist either. I sneaked out of the small women's shelter where she was born in the small hours of the morning.

"You won't need one," he says.

The SUV slows. I look out the window to see a small aircraft, only three windows across the side. "This is what we're taking? Are you sure it's safe?"

He gives me a small smile. "It's safe, little bird. And even better, they don't ask questions."

The words are pointed, reminding me that I'm asking too many questions. But I understand the deeper point, that we need someone who will let me fly without paperwork. And hopefully no one will answer questions if someone asks about a girl with long blonde hair.

The plane takes off within an hour. I'm clinging to the seat, my knuckles white. Delilah fusses at the loud noise of takeoff, the strange feelings in her ears. Her cry is drowned out by the roar of the engines.

Only Luca looks unaffected by the rush and the noise.

He turns to dig through a small compartment on the other side of his seat. He finds an empty glass and a bottle of water. Pouring only an inch into the glass, he turns it this way and that near the window. A sliver of rainbow appears on the carpet at my feet.

Delilah quiets, noticing the colorful light. Luca entertains her through the takeoff, the incline, making rainbow shapes on the floor until our ears are clear. By the time the sound of the engines level off, I can hear her squeals of delight.

"More," she says. "Wah more!"

It's only a matter of time before she demands the cup itself. Not for drinking, but to play with the small amount of liquid, sticking her hand into the glass, splashing it, spraying droplets at me until I have to laugh.

I'm still laughing when I turn to Luca. The seriousness of his expression makes my smile fade. Suddenly I'm self-conscious, wondering how I look playing with a one-year-old. Do I seem like a child myself? Like a backward country girl on a plane for the first time?

Do I look like a victim?

I'm all those things, but maybe, just maybe, if we make it so I don't have to run, I can be something more.

Chapter Eleven

THE CARAVAN OF luxury SUVs that carry us away from my apartment felt extravagant. The small private plane feels extreme—but they're nothing compared to the private jet that awaits us in Seattle. It's sleek and gleaming, with the word *Pajarita* across the side. A man in a suit and dark sunglasses waits beside metal stairs. Delilah has been fussy since halfway through the drive, not at all pleased to be confined to a seat when she wants to roam.

"We have a few minutes before takeoff," Luca murmurs.

He pulls the car seat away from me and heads up the stairs.

I follow him, my eyes widening at the inside of this plane—all wood paneling and plush carpets. The seats aren't stacked together like the small plane. Instead they're arranged in a casual circle, each with a large headrest and wide leather arms.

It's a relief to kneel in front of Delilah's seat where Luca sets her down, to focus on something mundane like stroking her hair into place, unlatching her seat belt. She springs up with a wordless exclamation of gratitude.

"Thank you," I murmur, unable to look at Luca.

I knew that my apartment was small and dingy, but this is a whole new world. What did Luca think when he saw my broken car and the sleeping mat? I must look pathetic to him.

"Hey." He touches my arm, and I look at him. "I know we're the reason you don't have a home. Because we showed up with fucking—with guns blazing. And then I took you."

Doesn't he understand that he saved me?

Delilah grasps the edge of the leather seat, pulling herself into a wobbly stand. She uses it as leverage to edge toward the back of the plane. A shiny mirror at the back is her goal.

"Stay here, baby," I tell her.

Luca glances down. "Everything in here is safe to fly. She won't get hurt."

A flush burns my cheeks. "I'm more worried about her breaking something."

"Let her."

"Won't Ivan be angry?"

"I doubt he'll care. It's my plane."

I take in the luxurious surroundings with fresh eyes. I knew that there was money to be made in the criminal underworld. Otherwise why would anyone do it? I didn't realize that Luca had this kind of wealth. Muscle, yes. Pure force.

What had he done to earn this kind of money? "How many people have you killed?"

His chuckle is low, unoffended. "More than my share, but I earn most of my money through fights. Big money fights, sponsorships. And betting, when I'm not in the ring."

"Oh. Then why do you—" I bite my lip, remembering it's none of my business. Girls were slapped across the face for asking questions in Harmony Hills. Living on the run brought me out of my shell by necessity, but I can never forget the pecking order.

His eyes darken. "You can ask me anything, Beth."

Already he has shown me more tolerance, more kindness than any man I've ever met. But his hands are huge, his arms bulging. His entire body weighs more than twice mine, hard packed and built to fight. If he ever decided to teach me a lesson, I wouldn't survive it. "Okay."

"Then why do I work for Ivan?" he asks, his

voice droll.

I wring my hands together. "You don't have to answer."

"Technically you didn't ask." He nods toward one of the wide leather seats. "Did you see the name of the plane?"

"Pajarita," I say, not knowing what it means.

His eyes darken. "Little bird. I named it after you."

My heart thuds heavy in my chest. Something this huge, this luxurious—after me?

He gives me a small smile. "Do you want anything to drink?"

As soon as he mentions the word, my mouth feels parched. A desert. I take a seat, feeling out of place in the plush armchair. I shove my hands between my knees, holding myself tightly. *Pajarita.* "Water, please."

He walks to the bar, a counter above where Delilah is blowing kitten-breath clouds on the mirror. He stirs around in the fridge before pulling out a clear bottle. He brings me back a glass.

"Thank you," I whisper before taking a sip. Bubbles tickle my nose.

Even the water is different here.

He takes the seat across from mine, our knees

almost touching when he reclines. "What do you think I'm going to do to you?" he asks, his voice mild.

My knuckles turn white as I clench the glass. I force myself to relax. "What do you mean?"

"You fought me tooth and nail when I took you from Harmony Hills. And you were ready to fight me again last night when we were alone in that shit hole—in your apartment. That's the Beth I know, but this morning you've been the picture of obedience. Tell me what changed."

When I fought him, I thought I could get away.

I thought I could keep Delilah safe on my own. I learned a long time ago never to rely on a man, never to trust him, never to believe that he wouldn't hurt you if he got mad. And Luca is so big and so strong it would be even worse.

Then he found me at the Last Stop, saving me in my final moments. Which meant my brother would have found me eventually. No matter how careful I am, they always catch up.

I choose my words carefully, knowing I can't risk insulting him. "I appreciate you helping me and Delilah. That's all I can focus on, keeping her safe. And you're helping me do that. Why would I fight you?"

Unless he wanted to hurt Delilah. I would turn into a lioness if he laid one of those large hands on her. I cringe, imagining the backhands I got when I was little. Those men hadn't been half as big as him.

"They fucked you up good," he says, his voice low enough that Delilah can't hear.

I flinch. "It's not a nice place."

"And I'm not a nice man," he says, as if acknowledging the conclusion.

"You've always been good to Delilah." And that's all that matters. That's all that can matter now. My brother would hurt me, but he would take Delilah away. And that means that I choose Luca, even if he requires my body as payment.

He leans forward, touching two fingers to my knee. I'm wearing jeans, but the feel of him burns like a brand. "I liked the Beth who fought me. You look like you're made of glass, so damn fragile a harsh wind could blow you over, but that's not true. I saw it when you stood in that office holding a rifle as big as you were."

A shudder works through my body. I contemplated hurting Leader Allen so many times. Every afternoon, our daily prayers. His wrinkled face above me, flushed red, panting.

Then when Candy brought those dangerous

men back to Harmony Hills, I knew that was my chance. My only chance to escape. And I took it.

"I've never been more scared in my life."

He laughs softly. "You were a goddess. And the strongest woman I've ever met."

He must have met so many women—beautiful, confident women. And of course he's seen Candy. Our looks are similar, both blonde, both slender. But she has wide eyes and full lips, curves in all the right places. "I'm not anything special."

"You wanted to know why I worked for Ivan. We met when we were kids. Both stupid, fucked up—sorry. Both of us dumb kids who wanted to get out of the *barrio*. He lived in a group home, parents long gone. I still had my mom at home. She turned tricks to keep food on the table."

Sympathy clenches my heart. It's hard to imagine this large man as a small boy, vulnerable to the cruelties of the world. "I'm sorry."

"Don't be. It made us tough. Forged in fucking—forged in fire. Like you, Beth. That's what I see when I look at you. A goddamn mirror."

My breath halts. "Me?"

"You and me, we're the same."

I swallow hard.

The sound of a cabinet door thumping draws

my attention to the far end of the plane. Delilah tugs on a door, but it's caught by some kind of lock that must keep it closed during flight. Her black curls shimmer under the ambient lighting, a dark angel.

She doesn't look anything like her father, at least not how I knew him—old and deranged. It would be a comfort to imagine that she was implanted by God, but I know better. Despite what Leader Allen preached, God never lived in Harmony Hills.

"I learned not to fight," I whisper. "Not to speak. Not to breathe when he didn't want me to."

The creak of leather lets me know Luca leans forward. "I'd kill that fucker all over again if I could."

Maybe we are the same, because I would too. "I don't want to be quiet anymore."

"No," he agrees gently. "Don't stop fighting me either."

Chapter Twelve

I'VE NEVER BEEN to Tanglewood, the city where Candy hid after she left Harmony Hills. All I know is what she's told me—the strip clubs, the gambling. The fighting rings where Luca spends his nights.

My heart thuds, a heavy beat. Working my way through the small cities has been hard enough. Learning the street signs, the strange customs that everyone knows but me. Counting money. Buying food. Every single step has been a steep climb.

Now I'm going to the biggest city I've seen, the darkest.

We find another string of black SUVs waiting outside when we land. They drive us through the city, which alternates between mansions and tenements, skyscrapers and gutters.

Ivan's house is like a castle in the center of the city, an urban fortress with high stone walls and sleek black cameras nestled into corners. Candy meets me on the front steps, eyes glistening with tears.

"Oh my gosh," she says, her voice awed. "She's beautiful, Beth."

Delilah resisted going back in her car seat for takeoff, but the rumble of the engine put her to sleep immediately. Now she blinks up at Candy, eyes wide and hazy.

"Thank you," I say, flushing with nervous pride. Motherhood isn't something I ever wanted for myself. I never imagined a happy home because I knew that was impossible. Duty. Pain. Those were the things that led me here, but I can't regret it. Not when I look at the trust in her dark eyes.

Candy pulls us inside, where marble floors expand for miles and chandeliers twinkle overhead. Luca excuses himself to look for Ivan, leaving me in a living room that could fit a hundred people.

"This place is like a palace," I say, my voice hushed.

She laughs, the sound knowing. "Pretty different from the Great Hall."

The Great Hall was kind of a joke, even among the true believers. There was nothing great about the dirt floors and the whitewashed walls.

Bars on the windows made it look more like a prison than a gathering place.

"I'm afraid to breathe," I admit. And unlike the plane, where flight safety had made it somewhat babyproof, there's plenty that's breakable here.

"Luca called and let me know that you were coming," she says. "I got a room ready for you upstairs. And my friend Honor's nanny is coming over tomorrow to help get the rest of the house prepared. She'll be staying with us for a couple weeks to help me out."

My heart clenches, thinking of leaving Delilah. It's been hard enough leaving her with a babysitter when she's asleep so I could work. This will be days. "Are you sure this is okay?"

"Of course," she says with a wink. "It's an honor having the blessed one in our house."

I make a face. "Not you, too."

"Hey, I think it's cool that the savior's a girl. It was time for a change."

Pulling out a plastic toy that plays light and sounds, I distract Delilah from our conversation. Delilah examines the familiar toy with an unimpressed sound. Then she half scoots, half crawls over to a potted plant, grasping at the wide green leaves overhead.

"I don't want her hearing about any of that."

Candy's expression softens. "I know it was messed up, but it's part of her history. It's definitely part of *your* history."

"I wish," I mutter. "That history has a way of following me around."

"We'll keep her safe, Beth."

Cameras. Walls. Will it be enough? "I can't lose her. I just…can't."

Tears prick my eyes. I put the heels of my hands to my face, trying to keep from crying. A soft touch on my shoulder shatters me. Comfort. Kindness. *God.*

I try to turn away, but Candy doesn't let me. She pulls me close, and I cry against her body, her breasts cradling me, her arms encircling me. I cry for getting attacked outside the Last Stop, for giving birth in a low-rent women's shelter. I cry for the little girl I once was, trembling and alone on a dirt floor.

"We'll keep her *safe,*" Candy whispers fiercely. "I won't let her out of my sight. And no one will know she's here. All they'll know is that you're in Chicago."

"Bait," I whisper, my voice thick.

"Trust Luca. He cares about you more than you know."

I pull away, retreating, hiding my face behind a fall of blonde hair. "You know what he wants from me."

"What's wrong with that?" she asks, her tone playful.

My nose scrunches. "You know what's wrong with that."

She smiles gently. "I know more than you think I do. I know that being with Luca won't be anything like what happened in Harmony Hills. And I know that he went crazy when you disappeared. He cares about you."

"It's a game to him."

"Maybe, but Ivan insisted that he forget about you. We have more important things to worry about, all that jazz. And you know what Luca said?"

We met when we were kids. Both stupid, fucked up—sorry. Both of us dumb kids who wanted to get out of the barrio. "What?"

"He told him to go fuck himself."

I flinch and then smile. "That sounds like Luca."

"Not before you. He was content to take orders as long as Ivan watched his back. They worked together for a long time without any problems. Then he meets you."

"And he kidnapped me," I murmur.

"He saved you." She knows what it was like there more than anyone.

"I'm grateful to him," I admit. "And I guess there's some part of me that's interested. But the most important thing in my life is Delilah. It has to be her. I'm not sure I can be with a man at all, especially one whose entire life revolves around violence."

Her hand touches mine. "Beth, our lives revolved around violence."

And mine still does. "I can't make it stop," I whisper.

"Luca will help you."

Luca will help me and hurt me. He'll use me in every way until I don't know where I end and he begins. That doesn't mean I shouldn't be wary. He's more dangerous than Leader Allen ever was. "You have to promise me something."

"Anything," she says promptly.

I glance at Delilah, who's scooted back to her toy. A Mozart sonata plays through the plastic speaker. My voice drops. "If I don't come back, you'll take care of her as your own."

She gasps. "No."

"Promise."

"You'll come back. Of course you will."

Except she can't be sure of that. I can walk into the crosshairs when it means keeping Delilah safe. I could walk through fire for her. I just need to know that she'll be taken care of if I don't come back. "As if she's your own child."

She looks away, her lower lip trembling. For the first time since she left Harmony Hills, she doesn't look self-assured. She looks like the young woman we both really are, forced to grow up too soon. "She's my sister, you know," she murmurs. "Both of us came from the same man."

I shiver. "I know."

"Besides, I owe you. If I hadn't run away, it would have been me in those prayer sessions. It would have been me with a baby."

Shame coils inside me. "I hated you for that."

Her eyes turn glossy with tears. "I'm so sorry."

"I hated that I couldn't go with you. That I wasn't strong enough or smart enough to run away like you." It was a hollow kind of hate, weak and brittle.

Her mouth drops open. "Strong enough? God, Beth. I wasn't strong enough to stay. I couldn't stand the thought of him touching me, not for anything. So I ran, not knowing if I'd survive. Not knowing or even caring who had to substitute for me. That was weakness, not strength. You're the strong one. You're made of freaking steel."

My throat feels thick. That's what Luca said, but I didn't believed him. He didn't know everything that happened in Harmony Hills, and I prefer it that way. I don't want to see the change in his eyes when he knows exactly what was done to me.

Candy knows. And she thinks I'm strong.

"Promise," I whisper.

Her nostrils flare. "I promise."

Relief flushes through me, swift and cool. "Thank you."

"She's my flesh and blood. I would always take care of her. It's an honor, not an obligation. But you—God, you're me. You're everything that I am, that I've been. Come back, Beth. I know you'll come back."

Chapter Thirteen

Part of me expects Luca to have sex with me as soon as we were alone.

And that secret part of me even longs for his heat, his unexpected tenderness. Longs for that sense of comfort I drew from his larger body curved around mine like that night in my apartment.

But he doesn't touch me in the black Escalade that takes us to the Tanglewood International Airport. He doesn't touch me on the private jet we take to a small Chicago airport, a mile expanse of runway and flat green enclosed by city glass all around. And he doesn't touch me on the limo ride into the city. If anything he seems to grow colder with every mile we take toward downtown.

Finally the frosty silence is too much for me. "Did I do something wrong?"

He glances at me, surprise flaring briefly. "Why would you think that?"

Maybe Candy told him that I was afraid of

him. I don't think she would do that to hurt me, but she might have been trying to help. "You seem different. Angry."

Dark eyes study me. "You haven't done anything wrong."

"Oh. Then why—"

"We'll stop by the hotel. I'll get you checked in and you can rest in the room while I'm gone."

Alone.

Maybe that would be a relief to some people. You're never alone in Harmony Hills, not even in sleep. And definitely not in those private prayer sessions I still experience in my nightmares. When I escaped, I was with Candy for a little while. Then Delilah. I don't know how to be alone. The silence cracks me like a hammer to glass.

"Where are you going?"

"To the gym. I need to check in with some of my team. And I need to start training."

For the fight. Because that's what he does—he hits people. And he gets hit. "Can I come with you?"

It will be even worse now that I'm missing Delilah. Candy will take good care of her, but that knowledge does nothing for the hole in my heart.

His eyes narrow. "It's a rough place."

"I worked at the Last Stop."

He quirks a smile. "Yeah. I guess you can handle yourself."

Until the end. I desperately needed Luca's help then. But I don't think anyone will attack me when they know he's in the vicinity. I may not trust him completely. I have a lifetime of experience telling me that men are dangerous, that violence breeds violence. But I know he won't let anyone else touch me.

In that way he has something in common with Leader Allen.

He had been possessive, too.

Even though Luca warned me about the gym, I'm still surprised when the limo glides to a stop in front of a warehouse. If it weren't for the faint light pressing through grime-coated windows, I would have thought the place abandoned.

It doesn't look much better on the inside, the walls sprayed with something that looks like cotton from far away, a large expanse of concrete broken by squares of thin, fraying mats. Colored duct tape creates divisions in the massive room, making it clear that the practice isn't haphazard even if it is low budget.

I expected rough men like Luca, but in a gentile setting. Something with granite and leather. This is a stark contrast to the luxury with which he travels.

Luca gives a low laugh beside me. "Thinking of backing out? I can have the driver take you to the hotel."

And sit in a cold room by myself. "No, thank you."

"MMA is only barely legal in Chicago. And there are a lot of restrictions. To keep fighting the way we do, with this kind of money on the line, they've kept it underground."

"Oh, so that's why it's so…"

"Jacked up?" he offers.

"I was going to say stark."

He snorts. "I'll be here a couple hours. You can sit on the bleachers over there. If anyone tries to talk to you, just tell them you're with me. Any questions?"

"One. If this fight is underground, how are you sure that my brother will hear about it?"

Appreciation flashes through his eyes. "Because the purse is the biggest. The prize. And that means the best fighters come out for this. Whether you're in the fight scene or not, people come to the after party. It's a free-for-all. We'll set a trap for him there."

"Oh." An underground fight and a party seem so far removed from our old life at Harmony

Hills. My brother, Alex, and I had never been close. He'd been a true believer long before I had been forced to be Leader Allen's personal attendant.

"He'll be there," Luca says, sounding certain. "If you're a dirty motherfucker—sorry. If you're mixed up with a bad crowd, you'll hear about it."

I manage a wan smile. "I guess you can swear now that Delilah isn't here."

"You don't like it."

It's a shock to realize he knows that about me. That he can see right through me. "Sorry."

"Don't be. It's a shit—a bad habit. And the fact that I'm joining the fight this late in the game will make all kinds of news. People have been training for six months."

My eyes widen. "And the fight is next week?"

He cracks his knuckles, looking like some kind of Spartan warrior. I can imagine him in gold and red armor, fierce in the face of catapults and arrows. "I've got some ground to make up."

I blink. "But if you usually fight, why weren't you already signed up for the fight."

"I was looking for you." He turns his head away, shielding his eyes. "Besides, I've been trying to fight less."

My heart clenches. "You don't like it anymore?"

Then he looks back at me, showing every vicious thought, every carnal desire for violence. "I love it."

"Then why do you want to stop?"

He nods toward the bleachers, where a few other women have set up shop with shiny phones and smoothies in Styrofoam cups. "Have a seat. I'll try to keep it quick today."

"Wait." I put my hand on his arm, amazed anew at the incredible strength that flexes beneath my palm. "You shouldn't fight for me. It's dangerous. And you haven't trained enough."

"Have a little faith," he says, gently chiding.

"I lost my faith a long time ago," I tell him honestly.

He sizes me up. "Yeah. I guess you did, little bird. Well, rest easy. Fighting's in my blood. This is what I was born to do. And you're the best reason I've ever had to do it."

Chapter Fourteen

I'M NO STRANGER to violence.

It's still a shock to see Luca in the ring.

There's blood and sweat, maybe spit, some tears as his opponent's nose makes a horrifying crunch. When Luca said *training,* I thought he meant push-ups and squats. Maybe some carefully contained pretend fights with protective padding.

Instead he's wearing nothing but shorts slung low on his hips, gloves on his hands, and a mouth guard. The fight doesn't seem to have rules. Trainers stand on either corner, hurling encouragement that sounds more like insults. Other fighters stop their training to watch Luca work. He takes out one man, then another. Then another.

"He'll be okay."

The voice startles me, and I turn to see a slender woman with brown hair and dark eyes. She's sitting on the bleachers a couple rows back, a book folded open beside her.

"You look a little tense," she says with a sympathetic smile. "Colin will take good care of him."

I glance back at the ring, looking closer at the rough man outside Luca's corner. "Colin?"

"He's working with Luca. I saw you come in with him."

"Oh. He's a trainer?"

"Kind of. He used to fight. Now he trains fighters, but he's real selective about it." She grins. "None of the other trainers wanted to work with Luca, considering how little time he had. But that's the kind of challenge Colin likes."

My eyes widen. "I didn't realize he'd be so far behind. Are you sure he'll be safe?"

"For training, definitely. The fights can get dicey."

I'm here to prevent violence. Not to cause it. "I told him he shouldn't."

She laughs. "If he's anything like Colin, he won't budge once he gets an idea in his head. I'm Allie, by the way."

"Beth," I say, feeling sheepish. She assumes that I'm with Luca, like we're dating or something. What would she think if she knew Luca was only doing this to protect me? To protect Delilah? That he risked his safety for me?

"Are you new in town?" she asks.

"Very. We haven't been to the hotel yet."

Her mouth drops. "I can't believe Luca brought you straight here. I'm going to have to talk to him. Or maybe just smack him for you."

"It was my idea," I say quickly. "I didn't want to wait alone."

She softens. "Well, feel free to talk to me while you're here. Once the guys get into this fighting stuff, they're in their own world. Us girls have to stick together."

I don't want to get close to someone. Don't want to feel hope, only to be disappointed again. But the allure of friendship pulls too strongly. "Thank you," I say, feeling shy.

A little girl with a pink tutu and a ponytail hops up the bleachers. I can't tell how old she is—maybe six. Maybe seven. "Mama! I'm hungry. Can I have a pretzel? Is it time to go? Ms. Ruby said she would braid my hair, but I like a ponytail better."

Allie's face lights up with a love so bright it almost hurts to see. "Hey, Bailey. Look who I found. This is Ms. Beth. She's here with Luca, the fighter your daddy is working with."

The little girl makes an *o* with her mouth. Her cheeks flush pink. "Hi."

Is this what Delilah will look like when she's

older? She has the same dark hair, straight and thick, unlike Delilah's lush curls. They have the same wide eyes and baby-pink lips. My muscles feel tight, but I manage a smile. "Nice to meet you, Bailey."

Then the little girl is back to tugging on her mother. Allie laughs while she extracts an apple. "Eat your fruit and then you can get a pretzel from the stand. I'm not sure when Daddy will be finished, so maybe you and I can stay for another twenty minutes. Then we'll go home and have dinner. Okay?"

"Okay!" Bailey skips off, the picture of childhood innocence.

It should look wrong against the backdrop of harsh concrete and violent men. But even their cold expressions soften when she skips by, crunching into her apple with vigor. She's completely at home, completely comfortable. Completely safe.

"That girl," Allie says in a rueful tone. "Do you have any?"

My throat sticks. "One. She's younger than Bailey. Twelve months."

"Ohh, still a baby. I miss Bailey being that young." Then she makes a face. "Though I wouldn't go back to that time for anything."

Even though her voice is light, I sense that

she's seen real darkness. I don't want to ask, but I'm drawn to the shadows. They ground me. They remind me of home.

"Colin mentioned that you were going through a hard time," she says softly.

The admission is torn from me. "I can't seem to get away from it."

Her eyes look older than her years. "You don't have to tell me the details. If it helps you to know, I don't mind telling you a little of my story. Colin isn't actually her daddy. We met four years ago, when I was still struggling."

Bailey's childish confidence takes on a new depth as I realize she's already experienced loss. Grief. The way Delilah's experiencing it, before she's even old enough to know. "What happened to her father?"

"He was…a troubled person." She winces. "I'm not supposed to downplay it. He did bad things. I still don't like to go as far as saying he was a bad person."

An unexpected comfort fills me. "I know exactly what you mean."

The feelings I have for Leader Allen are complex, layered. I despise him, but I respect him. And I definitely fear him. In the world he built, what he did to me wasn't even wrong. It was his due. And even though I'm glad he's dead, sometimes I miss him too.

She gives me a sad smile. "Maybe it would be easier if I could just hate him and forget him, but he's always there. When Bailey smiles a certain way or sneezes—and it reminds me of him all over again. I can't escape him."

The same way I see Leader Allen in my baby girl. "So what do you do?"

Allie seems so at peace. So happy. If I could find just a small piece of that ease, that security. If I could look even half as serene as she does…

"Mostly I forgive him."

Chapter Fifteen

Luca showers before he comes to me, blood trickling in pale rivulets from a cut on the side of his head. I look through the little compartments in the back of the limo until I find a napkin. I fold it once and reach for him.

He freezes. For a long moment I think he'll refuse.

Then he bends his head, almost princely as he receives my touch. I press the thin cloth against him, gentle in the face of his wound. His skin is hot and pulsing beneath my hand, body still flushed from the gym.

He might be a lion, lethal and wild, but he's my lion.

And I want him on my side.

"I can't believe you fought so hard."

He takes the napkin from me, his smile more like a grimace. "Sorry. Figured you'd rather stay at the hotel than see me like that."

"No, it was…" I'm not sure how to describe

his fighting. Brutal. Beautiful. "You were so skilled out there. Allie told me that the other trainers wouldn't work with you."

He laughs. "They didn't want me on their record if I got my ass handed to me."

"You beat eight guys in a row."

"Yeah, and I bet they're feeling pretty fucking—pretty stupid right about now."

I had to smile. Swear words used to make me flinch, but I'm getting accustomed to them. Like getting a tan when you've been out in the sun a lot. Soon they might not bother me. "Serves them right."

"I'm glad I'm working with Colin. He's tough. Straightforward. That's what I need this close to the fight. Because those guys were just the beginning."

And already bruises bloom along his cheek. "Are you sure you should do this? What if we just told people you're going to do it, so the word gets to my brother, and then you can pull out before the fight?"

He looks offended. "And pussy out? If I say I'm going to fight, I'm going to fight. Besides, I want to see the look of shock on their faces when I take the title."

I want to tell him it wouldn't be weak, that

sometimes surviving is the only kind of strength that matters. That's the lesson I learned. And I think it might be the one Allie did too. But I know that a man like Luca can never embrace it. He's forged himself into too powerful a weapon to ever bow down.

The limo slows, and I glance at the tinted window. My breath catches at the black overhang that covers a shiny brass revolving door. Burnished-copper sconces line either side of the walkway. Close-set bricks form a walkway from the curb to the door.

It's an old-world style charm. An expensive charm.

A valet opens the door, looking unfazed by Luca's rough appearance. He changed into a T-shirt and jeans, faintly damp as if he dressed before completely drying off. He looks rugged and dangerous. We draw more than a few glances from the patrons inside, but the woman behind the desk doesn't even blink when he hands over his credit card.

"Your suite is on the eighteenth floor, Mr. Almanzar."

He takes the cards with a gruff, "Thank you."

"Wait," I say, halting. My past taught me to be afraid of men. To be afraid of *everything*. But I don't want to live in fear anymore. "Do you have a first-aid kit we could use?"

The woman glances at Luca, then back at me. "Of course. I'll have the concierge send one up with your luggage."

If he insists on fighting, then I'm going to insist on patching him up.

And I'm taking Candy's advice. I'll trust him and see what happens. It's a risk, but one I can make without jeopardizing Delilah. It's just him and me for the next week.

My last chance to see what's possible. Intimacy. *Sex.*

As for Allie's advice, that will be harder to follow.

Luca raises his eyebrow at me but doesn't comment. He turns to the woman. "And send up dinner while you're at it. Steaks, medium rare. Some wine."

"Of course," she says, looking both apprehensive and awed.

Only when we step into a mirrored elevator does Luca mutter, "I'm not dying."

"Then you won't mind if I wash your cut." I hold my breath, waiting for him to slap me.

After a shocked pause, he smiles—slow and sure. "This is the girl I found in Harmony Hills.

The one I dragged into the car and tied up in my hotel bed."

I felt reckless then. And powerful, even though I was his captive.

Because I finally broke free of Leader Allen. It had been an illusion, that freedom. Leader Allen followed me into my dreams, my memories. Even the pretty face of my little girl. And he sent my brother after me, a physical danger to rival the emotional pain.

Allie somehow escaped her past, but I wasn't sure I'd be lucky enough.

Forgiveness or not, there's someone out there who wants me dead.

"This is the girl who's terrified," I whisper.

He takes a step forward, crowding me against the elevator door. I feel smooth metal at my back, a vertical line where the doors will open. "Terrified and fighting anyway," he murmurs. "You and I have that in common."

He looked invincible in the ring. "You?"

"Every damn time. So many times I almost got numb to the feeling, but with you it all came rushing back. Twice as hard. Twice as long. Everything sharp and deep."

I'm breathing harder, aware that we have this in common too. When he's in the room, things feel different, more clear, more focused. As if I can count every vein in a petal, every speck of pollen in the center of a flower.

His head lowers. His lips are an inch away, his breath a soft caress. His shoulders block out the light from above, leaving his face in shadow. All I have are my memories, the bruises and the blood—the fierce protectiveness that I can take shelter in.

He's going to kiss me.

I'm going to let him. Kiss me. Touch me. Everything has been building to this.

A ding sounds from above us. The doors slide open, and I fall backward. Strong arms keep me from landing on marble, and I stand up straight on shaky legs. Luca's expression hardens. He's not about to kiss me anymore. And the disappointment echoes in my chest.

✧ ✧ ✧

THE SUITE HAS two bedrooms. Luca disappears into one room, slamming the door hard enough to keep me from knocking. I stand in the living room, unaccountably dejected. I should be grateful that he's not making a move on me. The training left no doubt that he's a violent man. Bloodthirsty. Lucifer himself—that's how I saw him at the beginning.

I know from the night in my apartment that he can be gentle, too.

My room is large, with a plush bed as big as my old apartment bedroom. Plus, there's a desk and a small sitting space. A bathroom just for me. It all feels oversize and uncomfortable, this much space. Like I'm alone even though Luca's in the same suite.

I find my luggage already brought upstairs and unpacked into the dresser. The hot water scalds away the traces of travel, the lingering remnants of aggression from the gym.

Candy gave me a phone before I left, so I call her. She gives me a play-by-play of Delilah's day since I left, including noodles and watermelon for lunch, arts and crafts with Candy's stash of burlesque glitter and feathers, and twelve readings in a row of *If You Give a Mouse a Cookie*.

I'm smiling with tears in my eyes. "I'm sorry. She loves that mouse."

"No, it's a good story. I explained to her about bodily autonomy and consent. The mouse may *ask* for a mirror next, but you don't have to give it to him."

I hold back a laugh. "She's barely one year old."

"You might have a point. But we learned way too late."

My smile fades. "Yeah. We did."

She clears her throat. "Anyway. Do you want to talk to her? Oh, you can read her a book!"

"Let me guess. She picks *If You Give a Mouse a Cookie.*"

"Ding ding. Should I point the camera at the pages so you can read it?"

"Ha! I had it memorized after the first two hundred times. Just turn the pages for me."

There weren't bedtime stories in Harmony Hills. Only Bible stories. Cautionary tales about women who made the wrong choice, who were tempted by sin. From the very beginning, Eve was tempted by the apple in the Garden of Eden. Is that what I'm doing here in Chicago?

Am I going to burn?

I wish I could forget every verse I ever learned, but I can't. They're buried too deep, imprinted on my soul. It's hard to tell where my thoughts end and the Bible begins sometimes.

Is that how it will be for Delilah, dreaming of mice? Will the stories she loves now torment her when she's older? Will she be tempted by sin? Maybe there's no escaping it, whether it comes in the form of an apple or a cookie.

Chapter Sixteen

In the morning I'm dressed and waiting in the living room when Luca emerges from his room wearing sweatpants, a T-shirt, and sneakers. He plans to abandon me to the hotel room; I can tell.

"I'm coming with you," I say.

He narrows his eyes but lets me come.

I spend the day with Allie and her adorable little girl, Bailey. It's a joy to watch her run around the unforgiving warehouse, her smile lighting up the whole place. She tells me about her ballet lessons with Aunt Rose and her hamster named Fred.

Allie and I discover we have something in common besides ghosts from our past. We both love baking. She runs a small catering service that specializes in baked goods for weddings, baby showers, and children's birthdays. I'm in awe of what she's accomplished, even with a little girl. It gives me hope for my future, that I can make something of myself besides a waitress at dive bars.

When I tell her about my pies, she offers to buy some from me. But I don't have a kitchen. And more importantly I'm not sure how long I'll be in town.

Only a week, if all goes well. And if it doesn't…

Well, if it doesn't go well, I won't be anywhere on earth.

Luca told the truth when he said yesterday was just the beginning. Today Colin pushes him harder, demands more of him, gives him meaner competition. By the end of the day Luca wavers on his feet. I have to bite my lip to keep from going to him when he steps out of the ring. I clench my hands into fists to keep from holding him, supporting him. Without asking I know he'd hate that sign of weakness. So I remain on the bleachers as he staggers to the showers, wondering how bad the real fight will be if this is only the second day of training.

Chapter Seventeen

I KNOW WHY he didn't worry about the small cut on his temple yesterday. He has ten cuts like it all over his body when we get back to the hotel suite. There are new bruises on top of the old ones, turning black and blue and yellow.

It's late by the time we leave the second day, dark outside. It's been raining while we were inside, the scent of wet city concrete rising up from the sidewalk, a little different in every city. Luca doesn't shower this time, and he shakes his head when I reach for him.

"I'm a mess," he mutters.

He means sweat and blood, but it's more than that. He feels more raw than before, as if the hits he took in the ring have reached inside him. My stomach clenches as I realize that this fight won't just hurt him physically. It's shining light into dark places.

Maybe this is why he doesn't want to fight anymore.

I let him keep his isolation through the lobby, where we get sideways looks from everyone, even the people behind the desk. In the elevator I stare at my reflection in the mirror—blue eyes bright with worry. Blonde hair darkened by rain left in the air.

When we enter the suite, he heads into his room and closes the door. To shower?

I set down my bag and my book more slowly, wondering what I should do. Wondering what I even *want* to do. The safest thing would be to leave him alone.

It's bedtime for Delilah, so I call her and read *If You Give a Mouse a Cookie*.

Twice.

Then I'm left to wander back into the living area. His door is still closed.

I stare at the plain white door as if the answers are embedded in wood. What would they tell me, if walls could talk? Would they say that he's a dangerous man, made more unstable by a day of violence? I would never consider knocking if Leader Allen were on the other side of that door. Rice feels uncomfortable for the first thirty seconds—and agony for the next twenty minutes. He could have whipped me bloody and it wouldn't have hurt more. I feel the echo of that torment on my shins.

Then I remember the haunted look in Luca's eyes. He has his own echoes.

His own torment.

My insides feel like they're made of liquid, quivering inside me as I approach the door. I raise my fist, trembling with trepidation, fighting back a lifetime of conditioning.

It's the memory of him holding me in my apartment that overcomes the pain of rice under my knees. He could have done anything to me that night. Hurt me. Used me. I couldn't have said no. I *wouldn't* have said no with Delilah's safety on the line. And all he did was hold me.

I knock.

Seconds pass with every heavy beat of my pulse. It thuds in my eardrums, louder than the silence that answers me. Is he asleep? Still in the shower?

Or what if his injuries are worse than anyone realized?

He might have a concussion, collapsed on the hotel floor. Or worse, he could have fallen in the shower, slipped from dizziness and exhaustion. I did this to him. I broke him.

Frantic, I turn the latch and push open the door.

He's lying on the bed, one arm slung over his eyes. There's blood staining his body, his sheets, the same as when he walked into the room. He hasn't showered. All he's done is take off his shirt and shoes. He's only wearing his sweatpants as he reclines on the bed.

He glances at me, eyes glassy. "Something wrong?"

"Oh God, you're hurt." I whirl and grab the first-aid kit from the mini bar, along with fresh towels and bottled water. He needs more than gauze. He probably needs a doctor, but as long as he's still conscious, he'll never agree to one.

He's scowling when I run back to his room. "It's nothing."

"It's something." I set the kit on the nightstand and dig through the bandages. "Can I call someone? The front desk probably has the name of a doctor. Or maybe Colin will—"

He makes a rough sound. "I'm not fucking dying, you know."

I flinch, holding a packet of alcohol swabs. "I'm sorry."

His eyes close, revealing how much pain he's in. "Fuck, I'm the one who's sorry. Bandage me, do whatever you want as long as you stop looking at me like that."

"Like what?"

"Like I'm going to hit you."

I turn away from him, breathing deep. I hadn't meant to reveal that much. Maybe he didn't mean to reveal that much either. "I'm just going to clean up your cuts," I say, my voice even. "It's the least I can do considering you're fighting for me."

There's a rustle of fabric as he sits up. "Go ahead."

When I face him again, I try not to meet his eyes. Instead I focus on the little squares of fabric to clean out his cuts. Fresh blood spills from the wounds, so I work efficiently to cover them with bandages. The white hotel sheets are already smeared with blood, but I want him to start healing.

There's a particularly bad bruise on his arm. It's bright red now, with red petals radiating out. The flower shape is one I recognize. "That one's deep," I say.

He narrows his eyes. "How do you know?"

Because I had my own flower bruises. "Isn't this intense for training so close to the main fight? Won't you be weaker with these cuts and bruises?"

His laugh is unsteady. "If cuts and bruises

made me weaker, I'd be dead right now. Guys like me, they make me stronger. Colin understands that."

There's only a little bit of tape left, and I make a note to call down to the front desk for more tomorrow morning. "Make me understand."

He looks away, his eyes distant. As if he's looking into the past. "Some guys, they fight for sport. They train every day and drink protein shakes. It's like basketball, only bloodier."

"But not for you."

"I learned to fight because I had to. And every bruise, it only makes me stronger. That's how I got to be where I am. That's how I survived."

I swallow hard, hearing what he's saying between the lines. Someone hurt him. Someone *hit* him as a child. "I'm sorry."

His voice gentles. "You understand about that, don't you?"

"Yes," I whisper.

"We're not so different, you and I."

"The bruises didn't make me stronger."

He shakes his head. "Not stronger with big muscles. With this thick head that no one can bash in, even though so many motherfuckers have tried. You're strong in ways I can only imagine.

Surviving on your own, with your daughter."

I turn my face away. "Surviving. That's not strength."

His rough hand turns my chin toward him again. "Surviving is the only thing that matters. And you are strong as fuck. Understand me, little bird? No matter how many times someone puts a cage around you, you never forget how to fly."

Both Luca and I were hurt when we were young. He turned hard and coarse. I turned meek. These were our survival strategies, and they stayed with us long after our abusers had gone.

My eyes burn hot with tears. But I don't want to cry, not now. Not when I feel the stirrings of hope after so long. I've always believed in Delilah, that she can have a real future, a better life. But it's been a long time since I believed in me.

"Thank you," I whisper.

"Don't thank me," he says roughly. "I don't want your gratitude."

And he doesn't want my bandages. "Get used to it."

His laugh fills the room. "And you aren't strong. You know how many people talk to me like that? You're a goddamn army of one."

My cheeks flush under his praise. And under his intense gaze.

Only now do I realize how close we are. We had to be when I was tending his wounds. Now I'm standing a foot away from him for no reason at all. This close I can see the ring of darker green around the center of his eyes. I can see the scar that bisects his eyebrow, one that looks centuries old, from a different lifetime.

I know that being with Luca won't be anything like what happened in Harmony Hills.

Is Candy right about that? I want to believe her.

I want to find out for myself.

"Luca," I whisper.

His lids seem lower now, half-mast across his green eyes. He's breathing harder, more than when I put rubbing alcohol against his open wounds. "Little bird."

And I know that he went crazy when you disappeared.

There's temptation between us. And sin. But there's something deeper too. It might be trust.

"You told me not to stop fighting you."

His lips turn up. The air seems to shimmer with challenge. "You gonna punch me? Gonna make me bleed after you patched me up so nice?"

"What if I don't want to fight anymore?"

Everything seems to still as I hold my breath.

Even the earth pauses on its axis, waiting for his reaction. Fearing it. Anticipating it. His voice burns like lava. "You need something from me, little bird?"

"Show me what it would be like. If I hadn't been scared of you in my apartment. If the elevator yesterday had just gone on and on, never stopping."

"I'm hard as a goddamn lead pipe, but I'm not going to fuck you."

I suck in a breath. "Why not?"

"Because I'm not going to be another man you're afraid of. I figure you've got enough of those. And I can't stand to see you look at me like you regret it after."

My lips press together, because I don't know if I'll regret it. If I'll be afraid of him, after it's done. I despised Leader Allen every single time. What could be different?

Luca's green gaze runs over my body, more blatantly, more leisurely than before. He lingers on the curves, and I feel his regard like a physical caress. His voice is thick. "I won't fuck you, but I will make you come."

The words shift something inside me, a boulder that blocked every physical sensation. It protected me, once. Now it feels like another cage. "What do you mean?"

"Pull down your jeans."

My hands feel clumsy as I fumble with the button and the zipper. I manage to push my jeans halfway down my hips, leaving only my panties to cover myself. I feel more naked than I ever did in Leader Allen's prayer sessions. Luca sees more than my body. He sees my desire.

"What next?" I whisper.

"Let me take care of you."

The words are like water, filling some parched-earth part of me.

His skin is tanned and scarred against the smooth paleness of my tummy. His hand looks large fanned over my panties. "How do you feel?"

Scared. Shameful. "Warm."

He laughs softly. "I'm burning for you."

I can feel it, the flames of temptation licking over my skin. He hooks a hand at my hip, turning me around. With the jeans across my thighs, I start to fall. He catches me, guiding me into his lap. I gasp at the sensation of him, hot and hard, cradling me.

He pushes his fingers beneath the waistband of my panties, and I freeze.

His breath caresses my neck. "Relax."

"I can't." My voice is strangled.

His hand dips lower, down between my legs. To the source of temptation, the center of sin. This is where Leader Allen punished me. I'm shaking, about to throw up. It's too much, too fast…

"What's your name, little bird?"

My breath comes in pants. "What?"

"Your name."

My eyes flutter closed. "Beth."

"And who am I?"

He's grounding me, pulling me back into the present. Away from my past. "Luca."

"I'm the one with my hand down your panties. I'm the one touching your hard little clit."

My hips move against his hand on the word *clit*. "Yes."

"Do you like it when I pinch you here?" He demonstrates be pushing his thumb and forefinger around a bundle of raw nerves. His forearm flexes against my belly seconds before pure electricity arcs through my body.

"Oh no," I whisper, fighting the waves, the wetness.

"Or do you like it soft?" His touch gentles to a mere whisper, the hint of sensation that somehow feels more powerful, more intense than actual pain.

An uneven moan escapes me. "Please. Please."

"I know what you like," he murmurs against my neck, nipping the tender skin. "You like it steady, don't you? Nice and even, like the tide against the shore. Let's find out."

He presses the heel of his hand to me, pushing in a long-remembered rhythm, flicking his rough fingers at the slick skin at my core. I jerk against him, shocked anew at the pure energy that courses between us, the new language he's teaching me.

Trust me, his touch says.

Yes yes yes, my body answers.

Beneath my lap I can feel him hardening, pulsing in time with his hand. It means I've tempted him. Shame is carved too deeply in my soul. "I'm sorry," I gasp. "I'm sorry."

"My name, little bird."

"Luca."

"Again."

"Oh, *oh.* Luca!"

His fingers work me with merciless intent, drawing shudders from my body, whimpers from my throat. He pushes me closer to the edge, so tight I'm going to burst. In a flash of clarity I know why Eve took a bite. I can feel the waxy skin of the fruit against my tongue, almost taste the aching sweetness of its flesh. It doesn't feel like *want* or *desire*. It's starvation as Luca shoves a ripe apple between my teeth.

"Don't stop," he says, his voice thick. "My name. Don't fucking stop."

"Luca," I whisper, almost sobbing. "Luca. Luca."

"Yeah." The word sounds like syrup, slow and sweet.

My whole body tenses against him, straining at the hardness, wishing for it. The fabric is in the way—my panties, his sweatpants. They might as well be steel bars. I can't reach him, my inner muscles clenching around nothing.

He pushes my hair aside, kissing the side of my neck, nibbling. Then his teeth grasp hold of my skin. He bites me, and the shock of it, the delicious pain of it, makes me scream his name.

His fingers flick me, deep down, and I convulse in his embrace, pleasure washing over me in rapid, frothing waves, stealing the oxygen from my lungs, drowning out every ounce of shame. For blissful moments I'm aware of nothing except the gentle rocking motion. It's him. He's soothing me, stroking my belly, moving me carefully even while his erection throbs against my back.

I drowse like that, slumped on top of him, boneless. My head lolls on his shoulder. "Luca," I whisper, my voice hoarse.

"That's fucking right." The tension in his voice runs over my skin, as rough as his calloused fingers.

My hips settle against him, squirming. "We can—"

"No."

"But you need—"

"This close to a fight, I need to focus."

Sitting up, I turn to face him. His face is drawn in harsh lines of stress. His eyes are a glittering emerald green. "Then why did you do that?"

"Because you wanted me to. Because you asked. Do you think there's anything I wouldn't do for you? Making you come is a goddamn privilege. And if you still want me once the fight is over, it will be my privilege to fuck you, too."

Chapter Eighteen

For the rest of the week I sit in the bleachers with Allie while Luca trains. And every night I patch him up. He might be a lion, but he's *my* lion. When I put aside the first-aid kit, Luca's rough voice tells me to pull down my pants. He reaches under my panties and touches me until I'm sobbing his name, gushing against his fingers, turning the fabric wet.

It's a strange and sensual purgatory that I could live in forever.

Judgment day comes too soon.

The morning of the fight, I wake up to find the hotel suite empty. There's a note by the coffeemaker. *Went in early for strategy session. Allie will pick you up before the fight.*

The fight doesn't start until tonight. Why didn't he bring me with him? Why didn't he wake me up if he needed to leave early? I remember what he told me—*This close to a fight, I need to focus.* And I'm a distraction.

At least I can call Delilah during the day.

I find her finger painting with Candy, her face smeared with pink war paint. "Mama!"

"Hey, sweetie," I tell her, my heart feeling full. I'll get to her soon. And we'll be free of the threat, free from my past. And then what? Where will we go next? "What are you painting?"

"Wainbow," she says, holding up a picture with colorful streaks.

"That's beautiful. And just what I needed to see today."

"Mama!" Her voice is demanding, and I hear the questions in it. *Why aren't you here? When are you coming back?*

"I miss you so much, baby," I tell her with a sigh. "This will be over soon."

At least I hope so.

Luca has told me a little of the plan.

Colin has a network of other fighters and ex-military guys stationed at the ticket entrance. Of course they've never seen him. Even Luca's never met him. So I worked with someone who contracts with the police force to create a sketch.

With any luck they'll apprehend him when he enters the stadium.

I'm a little nervous with the knowledge that I'll be close to him soon. Even if he doesn't make it inside, we'll be in the same city. In the same building. We might have already been, if he's stalked me here. I've been well insulated in the hotel suite and the gym—both heavily guarded places. And I've always had Luca at my side. Except now.

My breath catches. It would be the perfect time to approach me.

I gaze out the large windows overlooking the city. The buildings seem to go on for miles, highways running through them like arteries through muscle. Is he out there?

Or is he even closer?

The skin prickles on the back of my neck. With uncanny certainty I can feel him closing in. Maybe that's just paranoia. Or maybe Luca understands the darker shadows of the mind enough to predict this.

On jelly legs I cross the plush carpeting to look out the peephole.

And let out a startled squeak at the distorted view of a man on the other side. Not my brother. Wearing a suit, from what I can see.

"Ma'am?" he says through the door. "Are you okay?"

My heart thuds with lingering adrenaline. "Yes. Um...who are you?"

"West Hightower, ma'am. Sorry to startle you. If you give Luca a call, he can verify my identity."

Too late I remember that the elevator required a key card to open on this floor. I flip open the lock. "No, I'm sure you're—"

"Ma'am, I'd really prefer that you call Luca."

I blink, startled at his insistence. So I find my phone and call Luca, who confirms that he did send West Hightower, a private security consultant with Blue Security, to protect me while he's training. When we hang up, he sends me a picture of the man outside, not smiling, wearing a suit.

With a small laugh I open the door. "Wow, these are some serious security measures."

West doesn't smile. "We want to keep you safe, ma'am."

"Of course." My stomach falls, the ground rising up to meet me. "So I'm stuck here?"

"No, ma'am. We can go anywhere you need to. There's a car downstairs."

I glance back at the skyline. "I'd actually like to go for a walk."

West excuses himself to confer with the other guards on my detail. Apparently there are more than one. I feel like royalty or something. But it doesn't take long for them to sort out a plan of action. Then we're heading down the elevator to the ground floor.

Out on the street I glance to the left and then right. There are several little pizza shops and one with sub sandwiches. There's some kind of electronics store and a concrete park with a metal playground. I choose one direction at random and keep walking until I find what I'm looking for: a steeple.

It doesn't matter what denomination the church is. There's no place that worships like Leader Allen did except for Harmony Hills. And I don't believe him anymore—most of the time.

This is a Catholic church, with a long display of candles as I enter. Each one represents a different saint. Some are already burning, by whoever came in before me. I find the candle for St. Francis, who cared for the poor and the sick, who loved all creatures big and small, and light it with shaking hands.

The pews are made of a beautiful scarred wood, with small kneeling benches in front of them covered with burgundy leather. West tails me all the way to the church, but once we enter, he stands at the back, arms crossed behind him.

I walk down the aisle in my jeans and T-shirt, feeling out of place. I'm not fancy enough for the elaborate stained glass or altar made of marble. But I slip into one of the pews, kneeling on the padded bench. I bend my head and whisper the Lord's Prayer five times.

It's a comforting ritual. A painful one.

Does my brother still pray? Of course he does. True believers never stop.

"Do you need counsel, my child?"

I jump, almost falling off the narrow bench. Whirling around, I see a man in black cloth and a white square collar sitting behind me. How did he sneak up on me? Over his shoulder I see that West has gone.

"Father?"

"Yes, my child?"

"I don't know what to do."

His wrinkles deepen in a gentle smile. "That's what I'm here for."

I struggle with the words. "The things that I learned, the things that I was taught, they aren't right. They're not what Jesus taught. And now…now I don't know what to believe."

Part of me expects him to ask what I've been taught. Maybe if I were raised Baptist he could convert me to Catholicism. Instead he sighs, studying the golden cross with rheumy eyes. "A crisis of faith. Is that right?"

"Yes, Father." *So punish me, punish me. Make me hurt.*

"Sometimes I wonder whether I've followed the right path."

Surprise jolts me out of the past. "You do?"

"That's the lovely thing about faith. There's no science to prove it. No numbers to define it. We can't touch it or taste it. We're supposed to question it. That's what makes it faith."

"Then how do you decide what to believe?"

"I think about what will help me the most, what will help my flock the most. And I try not to judge other people for their beliefs. But most of all…most of all I try to forgive."

My breath comes faster. How could a woman of sin, proud and serene, come to the same conclusion as a man of God? "What if I can't forgive?"

The things Leader Allen did to me, I'll never really let them go.

"Then he must not deserve forgiveness," the priest says gravely. "But remember, you are not bound by anyone else's faith but your own. You can take what resonates with you and leave the rest. You can use what works for you. That's the beauty of faith."

I bow my head. "Thank you, Father."

We're silent a moment, communing in the acknowledgment of our mutual frailty, our fallibility in faith—but if I understand him, then it's supposed to be fallible. It's supposed to be frail. That's what makes it a miracle.

My knees are stiff by the time I stand. The priest still prays one row behind me.

I head down the aisle and look back. "Father?"

"Yes, my child."

"Why do you think Eve took a bite of the apple?"

He gives me a small smile. "You're asking about temptation."

"I'm asking about sin."

"I think she took a bite of the apple for the same reason you're asking me these questions. Do you call it disobedience? Or do you call it a crisis of faith? I call it yearning for knowledge. God gave you that curiosity, child."

It's a different interpretation of the Adam and Eve story I've been shamed with my whole life—a brighter one. Because God gave me this curiosity. He gave me the apple.

"Thank you, Father."

I turn to the back of the church, expecting West to be gone, half thinking he was some handsome fever dream my mind made up. He's standing as still as a statue, head bowed as if in prayer. I approach him quietly, not wanting to interfere.

He smiles gently. "Ready?"

"Completely."

I'm ready for knowledge, for sin. Two sides of the same coin. I want to know him in every way possible, including carnal intimacy. When this is over, I'm going to tell Luca how I feel. I'm going to ask him to stay with us, wherever we end up going. Because I'm curious about what we can become together. And I'm strong enough to find out.

Except as we pass the rows of candles, some lit and some not, the candle for St. Francis isn't burning anymore. A coincidence in a drafty old church?

Or was it snuffed out by someone watching me?

Chapter Nineteen

"THE FIGHT'S ABOUT to start." Allie yells to be heard over the roar of the crowd. The fight hasn't started yet, but half the people here seem drunk. They're screaming at each other, at the empty cage in the middle of the warehouse.

West and the man guarding Allie push through the crowd, making barely enough room for us to squeeze through. Our seats are near the front, which is a relief. I'm only steps away from the emergency exit. If I were in the center of the stands, I'm not sure I could breathe.

Of course this means I have a close-up view of the ring.

The warehouse has been transformed from a crude gym into some kind of party. The lights are dim, with colorful spotlights flashing over the crowd. Smoke fills the air. I can't see Luca anywhere, but he's probably off somewhere with Colin.

A man in a black-and-white checkered shirt

strolls the perimeter of the ring. A ref?

I lean close to Allie. "I thought these fights weren't legal."

Her gaze follows mine. "They still have rules. Even the hard-core fighters don't want anyone dying. That would make the authorities come around."

My eyes widen. "Dying?"

She presses her lips together, looking sheepish. "Sorry. Luca's definitely not going to die."

That kind of reassurance really has the opposite effect. "Do people die in these fights?"

Every second she takes feels like an eternity. "It's happened before. I mean, sometimes people have weak health. Or it's a freak accident. It can be dangerous, but in a fight like this, with so much scrutiny, they're taking every precaution."

I swallow hard. "What kind of precautions?"

"Searching for weapons."

My eyes widen. "People bring *guns* into the fight?"

"No, of course not," she says, but my relief is short-lived. "I mean knives. Or brass knuckles. That kind of thing. But it's definitely not allowed. Don't worry."

I'm worrying. Bad enough that Luca has to do something that reminds him of his past, that makes him feel unsettled, unsafe. That makes him feel like the little boy in the *barrio*. Bad enough that he'll be bruised and beaten at the end of the night, even if he wins.

But to think he might not walk away from the fight? Dread snowballs inside me.

She touches my arm. "Beth, I'm really sorry. Luca will be fine. I'm sure of it."

I take deep breaths, soaking in the thick air around me. "No, of course. You're right. Just…maybe distract me. Where's Bailey?"

"She's having a sleepover with her Uncle Philip. They have a new baby, and she loves to help out with her."

Some of my tension eases. "That's adorable. Do you ever think of having another one?"

A smile plays at her lips. "Actually…"

My eyes widen. "Are you serious?"

"We haven't told anyone except family yet, but…yes."

I reach over to give her a hug, unable to help myself. "I'm so happy for you."

She squeezes me back, holding on another minute. When she pulls back, her eyes are shining. "Thank you. I'm really happy—terrified, but happy. What about you?"

My laugh is unsteady. "Another baby? I can

barely keep up with Delilah."

Her gaze scans the crowd. "What about Luca?"

A lump forms in my throat. "What about him?"

"He could help you."

"A man like him isn't in it for the long haul."

She's quiet, a sea of serenity in the madness of the crowd. "I don't know. I think a man like him might be *exactly* the kind of man who's in it for the long haul."

"What kind of man is that?"

"The kind of man who knows a good thing when he's found it. The kind of man who'll hold on to it as long as he can."

I can't look at her or the crowd. I can only stare down at my hands as if they hold the secrets of the universe. Is there a God—and if there is, what does He think of me? Is it sinful to let Luca rub between my legs? Or is it the only heaven I'll ever know?

A roar comes from the crowd, and I look up to see Luca head toward the ring from the opposite side. He ignores the crush of people reaching for him, looking more fierce and intent than I've ever seen him. His eyes are hard black diamonds, glittering even from across the warehouse. He ducks between the ropes, Colin behind him.

And if you still want me once the fight is over, it will be my privilege to fuck you, too.

The memory of his words wash over me in a sensual rush.

Clamor drags me back into the present, a wild cheer as another man steps out—this one coming from the double doors right near us. He's built tall and thick, a brick wall. He's wearing a robe that leaves his face in shadow. Menace rolls off him, almost palpable. The only thing I can see through the darkness are his eyes, flat and cold.

My stomach turns over with instinctive discomfort.

A man in a suit speaks into a microphone, rallying the crowd to louder and louder heights. The sound becomes waves, crashing over me. It's impossible to speak to Allie, even yelling. I can't even think with this much commotion around me, sweeping me up into its frenetic energy. It feels like the exorcisms Leader Allen would do, his violence turning the crowd into a mob. In fact, that's who the other fighter's eyes remind me of—Leader Allen's, hollow and reptilian. He takes off his robe, revealing ropes of muscle layered on top of each other. He's in the corner nearest me, so I can't see his face.

The only comfort is West, the guard, who stands a few rows back from me.

I'm grateful to Luca for sending him to guard me.

The buzzer goes off, and the fight begins.

Both men circle each other, throwing easy hits that aren't returned. They're testing each other. I've watched Luca fight all week. I know his style. He's holding back plenty.

Then suddenly everything shifts, and the other man lunges for Luca. A solid hit, which whips around Luca's large body. When he straightens, his lip is bloody—and there's a feral gleam in his eyes. As if that taste of blood is all he needed to attack.

Luca pulls a combination move that has the other man staggering against the ropes.

But he's up again and coming back at Luca. They're well matched, both of them at the top of their games. The best in this underground fighting world. Head to head. I cringe every time the other man lands a punch on Luca, wince when he takes a fall.

I'm close enough that I see the other man knee Luca's groin.

I call out as if I can somehow fix it.

Colin's shouting, his face a mask of fury. The

ref calls a time and gives the other man a warning. But if there was any doubt, now I know he'll fight dirty.

They wear each other down, both of them violent and ferocious. It's painful to watch, but I can't look away. This is the man I love—

The thought stops me cold. *This is the man I love.*

Do I love Luca? I'm not sure, but I can't stand the thought of him being hurt.

The other man has to head back to his corner. That's when I get a clear view of his face, a spotlight flashing over those features so like mine. *Alex.* My brother. My heart stops. How is that possible? No wonder the men working with Luca didn't see him. He's not a spectator.

He's a *fighter*.

Then something gold and shiny catches my eye. It's on the other man's hand. A ring? My stomach drops. No. Brass knuckles. He'll hurt Luca. He'll kill him!

I take a step toward the ring, determined to do something. I don't know if anyone else has seen them, but it's way too loud to hear anything. I have to help him.

A hand on my arm pulls me back.

West. He frowns at me, his mouth forming

words.

I yell at him. "Luca's in trouble. Brass knuckles! My brother!"

He doesn't understand, so I point to my knuckles. His eyes widen. He mouths the words, *Stay here.* And only because I think he's probably right do I listen. I'm afraid that if I climbed into the ring, I'd distract Luca—giving the other man the perfect opening. He needs real help, someone strong, someone who can fight.

West heads for the ring, but two security men block him.

He exchanges rapid words with them before shaking his head in disgust. He starts to turn away—where is he going? He's circling the ring, I realize, heading for Colin. Colin sees him coming, knows there's a problem, but he doesn't know what.

That's when Alex's fist comes up in the air, flashing the spotlight back in the crowd. Everyone can see the brass knuckles, but it's too late.

"Luca," I scream.

My warning is swallowed by the crowd. The other man's fist hits Luca's face in a spray of blood, and I scream again, wordless and horrified. No no no.

I surge forward, desperate to be near Luca, to

protect him.

The crowd surges forward, multiplying the chaos. The men who'd been guarding the stage area scramble, some heading into the ring to help, others mixing with the crowd. With the smoke and the shadows, it's impossible to see Luca.

An arm wraps around my waist, and I struggle, thinking it's another one of the guards with West. Maybe the man guarding Allie, maybe Allie herself. I fight, but the hold is like iron—it drags me back and back. We don't head to the seats, but instead out of the exit. The arm over my waist is covered in some kind of silky material. A robe.

I look over my shoulder, into the face of my brother. *Alex.*

Every part of me feels cold, the same desolate winter I felt in the prayer sessions. Oh God. He's wearing his robe again, somewhat disguised to the crowd. But no one's even looking at us. Everyone's focused on the ring.

"Luca," I scream again, this time my voice raw with hopelessness.

It doesn't matter. He can't hear me. He's down on the mats, his large body obscured as men crowd into the ring. Is he alive? I can't tell. I don't know. Then we're through the doors. They swing closed in front of me, blocking out the sight of

Luca. Turning down the volume.

"Let me go," I whisper. "Alex, please."

My brother's voice is grave. "I'm here to save you, sister."

Chapter Twenty

Alex drags me toward the exit, but there's already a crowd gathered. The doors slam open as paramedics wheel a stretcher inside. My brother makes a growling sound, before dragging me the other way. The only door left leads into a locker room.

He uses a loose pipe throw the metal handle to lock us inside.

"Alex," I say, my voice shaking. "What are you doing?"

"I told you," he says, pulling something around my wrists. "I'm saving you."

"You're kidnapping me."

He laughs shortly. "Kidnapping. One of the milder crimes I've been accused of."

"Leader Allen turned you into a monster."

"Leader Allen was the monster," he snaps.

My mouth closes. I hadn't realized he knew that. "He was."

"He deserved to die. I should have killed

him."

"Alex...if you think that, then why have you been searching for me?"

"To get you away from those...those heathens! Do you think they're any better, sister? They'll rape you and throw you away. I saw the way he kept you, never letting you out of his sight. Like some pet."

Like a little bird he had caged.

Except Luca had every chance to hurt me. Instead he wanted to heal me. "So you're going to keep me in this locker room forever?"

"Better here than with him," he snaps.

"He doesn't hurt me."

A makes a rough sound. "You sin with him. Tell me I'm wrong."

I realize Alex is like me—broken by our past, unable to shake the chains. We know that Leader Allen was wrong, but we can't forget all the lessons. "It isn't a sin."

And in that moment, I know it's true. Love can't be a sin.

My brother snarls. "I killed him so he couldn't touch you again."

I'm stricken. Is he dead? "You're sick."

He paces away from me. "Sick. Sick. Sick. That's what he called me. Sick."

I blink, confused. Alex was always the perfect soldier for Leader Allen. That's what he called them—soldiers. His spiritual army. "Who called you sick?"

"Leader Allen. And he was right. I'm disgusting."

I wriggle my fingers behind my back, but the rope is tight. I can't break free. "Why are you disgusting?"

"For what I want." His eyes plead with me. "For what I still want. I can't get away from it. The sin. *The pleasure.*"

I swallow past the knot in my throat. "Alex. Leader Allen hurt me. He…" My eyes close against the truth, but the darkness only makes it more real. "He touched me." I open my eyes again, seeing the same shame reflected back at me. "Did he hurt you too?"

"You don't understand," he whispers.

"What don't I understand?"

He comes and lays his head in my lap. "I wanted it."

"Oh, Alex," I whisper brokenly. "I'm sorry."

And I am sorry. Even if he killed Luca. I can't hate him for what Leader Allen turned him into. *Mostly I forgive him.* That's what Allie said to me. That's all I can do.

"Don't be," he snaps, rearing back. "The devil's inside me."

"Leader Allen's the only one inside you, whispering all those horrible things to you."

Alex's face is pale, making him look younger than me instead of older. "I'm gay, Sarah Elizabeth. He said that if I did everything he told me, that he could cure me. That he could fix me. But now he's gone and I'm still sick."

There's a bang on the door, so loud and fierce that we both jump.

"Beth!"

Luca's voice washes over me like salvation. He's alive!

Although he probably should be lying down, not running around a crowded warehouse. And he definitely shouldn't be chasing after my brother in his condition.

And I realize something else—Luca will kill him. Taking him in alive, turning him over to the authorities. Those things might have been possible if Alex was apprehended by one of the men at the entrance. Maybe even after the dirty fight.

But now he's kidnapped me. Luca will never let him live.

"Let me go," I say urgently. "It's only a matter of time until he gets in here."

Alex pulls out a gun. "You think I don't have a backup plan?"

My mouth goes dry. "Please, no."

He looks at me with such solemn sorrow, the crowds of religious furor clearing for a moment, and I know I'm seeing my brother for maybe the first time. "Do you really want him?"

I really want him, with every scar and shadow he comes with. "Yes."

His gaze lingers on the gun, contemplative, his hold turning sideways. "Then there isn't anything left on this earth for me to do, is there?"

Horror seizes me as I realize how he plans to end this.

"There's not just hope for her," I say, urgent as more banging comes from the door. I twist my hands, managing not to wince at the harsh burn against my wrist. If I strain, I can just barely reach the knot with my fingers. "There's hope for us too. You. Me. We can live normal lives, too."

He laughs, harsh and cold. "We'll never be normal."

I know that now. It was a false dream. I came from Harmony Hills, both the good and the bad. That's my history. We can't ever escape our memories, not really, but we can learn from them. And we can go on living.

"I know it won't be easy, but we can find a new faith. One that works for us. And maybe, with time, we can…" I close my eyes, knowing this is the answer. And the hardest thing I'll ever have to do. "We can forgive."

"You're lying," he snarls. "You're delusional."

"Maybe. Or maybe I finally learned the lessons. Not of Leader Allen, but the Bible itself. What it was trying to tell us all along."

Alex turns the gun to himself. "It's just an old book, Sarah Elizabeth."

The gun expands from half an inch to fill the whole room. It's all I can see, because for maybe the first time ever, I understand forgiveness. It's not only Leader Allen I need to forgive, not only Alex. It's myself. I don't only need to live for Delilah. I want to live for myself, for Luca. I want to live for the sake of living, for the beauty and the evil and every shade in between. I want to take a bite of the apple, because it's the only thing that matters.

"Call me Beth," I say gently, working furiously at the knot. "That's my name now."

"You can't just change your name," he says, pleading, hands sharking violently as he stares down the barrel. "You can't just go on with your life like none of it happened. Like it doesn't matter."

"It matters, Alex. It matters so much sometimes that you'd rather die than go on living. I understand that. And I'm grateful that I had Delilah to keep me holding on during those times."

His eyes are bleak. "And what do I have?"

The rope falls to the floor. "You have me."

I put my palm up, waiting. I won't fight him. I wouldn't win. He has to choose this—choose family, choose life. One breathless moment, then two. He sets the gun down on the floor and takes my hand.

The door bursts open.

Luca rushes into the door, looking like a wild bull on a rampage. He's covered in blood and bruises, his face twisted in a snarl. He'll kill Alex with his bare hands. He reaches him before I do, throwing a punch that sends Alex back into the lockers.

I throw myself in front of my brother, because sometimes you have to forgive. You have to make your own faith in this crazy world we live in. And I believe in Luca.

Chapter Twenty-One

Waves send music through the open window. The smell of salt floats in on the breeze. Three weeks in paradise and I still marvel at every moment. Hawaii is a land of ocean and lava, of sand and stone. A crack in the earth built for us. After my brother agreed to work for Ivan—a kind of criminal penance, after I got Delilah back from a tearful Candy, we made our own Eden.

"Slow," he says.

I feel like I've been waiting my whole life for this. And I don't have any patience left. I push my hips down, only to wince. He's too large.

"Slow," he says, sharper this time. His hands grasp my hips, holding them in place.

So far we've done everything but sex, again and again, in every position possible. He wanted to explore my body; he wanted me to explore his. Until I'm begging to feel him. There's an ache deep inside me that only he can fill.

I'm on top of him, knees spread wide over his hips. "I can't."

"We can wait, little bird."

"No, I want—I need—"

His laugh is unsteady. "I know what you want. But you'll get it when you're ready. And that means you taking me inside your body without pain."

I'm ready for him now. And being with a man this big would always hurt a little. I close my eyes and focus on the sensations, on the stretch. And then I do what he told me to—I go slow, sinking down on him, impaling myself by degrees.

When he's fully seated, shivers run over my skin.

My eyes fly open, meeting his green regard. "I love you," I whisper.

He doesn't seem surprised. "I know."

"How?"

"I knew in the hotel suite in Chicago. When I touched your pretty little clit." He demonstrates by rubbing his thumb over my clit. "You wouldn't have given yourself to me if you didn't love me."

I experiment with moving my hips, gasping at the thickness of him. "I offered myself to you at my apartment."

"That was different. That was payment."

I bite my lip. "What's this, then?"

His hands grasp my hips, and he thrusts up. "This is pleasure."

"It may be pleasure, but we still had a deal."

His expression grows dark. "I'd take you anywhere you want to go."

"And you'd leave me there."

He stills, his hands tightening on my hips. "I didn't promise."

"Could you do it? Would you leave me?"

A shudder runs through him. "I'd sooner rip off my arm."

"Good," I whisper, lifting myself and sinking down again. Because I had found my prince. He didn't have blond hair or a white horse. He had green eyes and a mean left hook. And he had slayed every one of my dragons. "Because if you left, I'd follow you."

He closes his eyes briefly, as if in pain. "God, Beth. *Fuck.*"

I smile, because Delilah's still with Candy and Ivan in their villa. She can't hear him swear. "Now say it."

His eyes narrow. "Say what?"

"You know what." And I roll my hips as punishment for making me wait. The way he gasps makes me feel powerful. I want to explore this newfound sensual strength.

He grits his teeth, flexing inside me. His eyes meet mine. "I love you, little bird."

And I realize that I'm not surprised either. "I know."

A rough laugh. "I've loved you from the moment you stood in that doorway with a shotgun in your hand. And I would have followed you anywhere. God help me, I still will."

I meet my lips to his, promising him without words that I'm here, that it's all right—that he might follow me, but I will lead him wherever we're meant to go.

Epilogue

The sweet ache of red bean paste fills the bungalow, wafting into the living room where I'm reading a book. A timer dings from the kitchen, and I cross to check on the buns. I learned how to make *Anpan* from the woman two doors down from me, a young woman with dreadlocks and a gorgeous island accent.

Mine aren't as good as hers, but the crust is golden and the red bean paste has caramelized where it's seeped from the bun. I pull them from the oven, moving them onto a rack to cool.

Then I push open the screen door to find my small family.

The island air lifts my hair around me, an ordinary magic. Small black gravel fades into pale sand. I hear them first—a small baby voice wafting in on the breeze. A lower voice answering her. Delilah took to the ocean like a mermaid, more comfortable swimming than walking. She'll go as far out into the sea as we let her.

Right now she's on land, her tanned legs dusted with a fine layer of sand. Her turquoise swimsuit has ruffles at her waist. A white cotton hat sits atop her dark curls, protecting the pale skin of her face.

Luca lounges opposite her, his skin dark after weeks on the island. His broad shoulders and muscled abs are covered with scars and faded tattoos, remnants of his former life. And on his chest, over his heart, are the fresh lines of a sparrow in flight.

"This is A," he says, drawing the letter in the sand with his finger.

She makes a slanted copy. "Apple."

He draws a B beside it. "B. B is for blueberries. And bananas. And bedtime."

She makes a sound of protest at the mention of bedtime. Her small fingers brush away the shape of the B. Instead she draws a heart. "Love," she says, though it sounds like "lub."

"That's right. Like your mommy loves you."

"I love."

He tweaks her nose. "And you love her too."

She stands, wobbling only slightly on the damp sand, before flinging her little arms around his neck. "Love you too."

Luca's eyes widen. Slowly his large hand

comes to cradle her back. I'm not sure he's ever been hugged by a child before. Maybe not anyone else but me.

The sight of them makes my heart squeeze.

Delilah sprints off toward her colorful plastic shovels and buckets, innocently unaware that she's left Luca looking shell shocked. He stands, almost gingerly, as if he's been hit by a ton of bricks. And maybe that would have been easier for him to bear than love.

I go to him, pressing my cheek against his hard chest.

His arms come around me, crushing me. "Thank you," he says, his voice thick.

The only reason we're free is because of him. "You saved me, Luca."

He presses his forehead against mine. "No, little bird. You saved me."

THE END

Thank You!

Thank you for reading Luca and Beth's story!

TO THE ENDS OF THE EARTH does standalone, but it also featured cameos from characters in both the Stripped series and the Chicago Underground series! If you're new to the sensual and dark USA Today bestselling Stripped series about a mafia princess who goes on the run and winds up in a strip club, you can start with Tough Love. And if you want to find out how Allie met her rough prince, you can start the gritty USA Today bestselling Chicago Underground series with Rough.

I'm so pleased to offer a sneak peek of my next release! THE PAWN is a brand new full-length dark contemporary novel about revenge and seduction in the game of love…

> *"Sinfully sexy and darkly beautiful, The Pawn will play games with your heart and leave you craving more!"*
>
> ~ Laura Kaye,
> New York Times bestselling author

Excerpt from The Pawn

WIND WHIPS AROUND my ankles, flapping the bottom of my black trench coat. Beads of moisture form on my eyelashes. In the short walk from the cab to the stoop, my skin has slicked with humidity left by the rain.

Carved vines and ivy leaves decorate the ornate wooden door.

I have some knowledge of antique pieces, but I can't imagine the price tag on this one—especially exposed to the elements and the whims of vandals. I suppose even criminals know enough to leave the Den alone.

Officially the Den is a gentlemen's club, the old-world kind with cigars and private invitations. Unofficially it's a collection of the most powerful men in Tanglewood. Dangerous men. Criminals, even if they wear a suit while breaking the law.

A heavy brass knocker in the shape of a fierce lion warns away any visitors. I'm desperate enough to ignore that warning. My heart thuds in my chest and expands out, pulsing in my fingers, my toes. Blood rushes through my ears, drowning out the whoosh of traffic behind me.

I grasp the thick ring and knock—once, twice.

Part of me fears what will happen to me behind that door. A bigger part of me is afraid the door won't open at all. I can't see any cameras set into the concrete enclave, but they have to be watching. Will they recognize me? I'm not sure it would help if they did. Probably best that they see only a desperate girl, because that's all I am now.

The softest scrape comes from the door. Then it opens.

I'm struck by his eyes, a deep amber color—like expensive brandy and almost translucent. My breath catches in my throat, lips frozen against words like *please* and *help.* Instinctively I know they won't work; this isn't a man given to mercy. The tailored cut of his shirt, its sleeves carelessly rolled up, tells me he'll extract a price. One I can't afford to pay.

There should have been a servant, I thought. A butler. Isn't that what fancy gentlemen's clubs have? Or maybe some kind of a security guard. Even our house had a housekeeper answer the door—at least, before. Before we fell from grace.

Before my world fell apart.

The man makes no move to speak, to invite me in or turn me away. Instead he stares at me with vague curiosity, with a trace of pity, the way one might watch an animal in the zoo. That might be how the whole world looks to these men, who have more money than God, more power than the president.

That might be how I looked at the world, before.

My throat feels tight, as if my body fights this move, even while my mind knows it's the only option. "I need to speak with Damon Scott."

Scott is the most notorious loan shark in the city. He deals with large sums of money, and nothing less will get me through this. We have been introduced, and he left polite society by the time I was old enough to attend events regularly. There were whispers, even then, about the young man with ambition. Back then he had ties to the underworld—and now he's its king.

One thick eyebrow rises. "What do you want with him?"

A sense of familiarity fills the space between us even though I know we haven't met. This man is a stranger, but he looks at me as if he wants to know me. He looks at me as if he already does.

There's an intensity to his eyes when they sweep over my face, as firm and as telling as a touch.

"I need…" My heart thuds as I think about all the things I need—a rewind button. One person in the city who doesn't hate me by name alone. "I need a loan."

He gives me a slow perusal, from the nervous slide of my tongue along my lips to the high neckline of my clothes. I tried to dress professionally—a black cowl-necked sweater and pencil skirt. His strange amber gaze unbuttons my coat, pulls away the expensive cotton, tears off the fabric of my bra and panties. He sees right through me, and I shiver as a ripple of awareness runs over my skin.

I've met a million men in my life. Shaken hands. Smiled. I've never felt as seen through as I do right now. Never felt like someone has turned me inside out, every dark secret exposed to the harsh light. He sees my weaknesses, and from the cruel set of his mouth, he likes them.

His lids lower. "And what do you have for collateral?"

Nothing except my word. That wouldn't be worth anything if he knew my name. I swallow past the lump in my throat. "I don't know."

Nothing.

He takes a step forward, and suddenly I'm crowded against the brick wall beside the door, his large body blocking out the warm light from inside. He feels like a furnace in front of me, the heat of him in sharp contrast to the cold brick at my back. "What's your name, girl?"

The word *girl* is a slap in the face. I force myself not to flinch, but it's hard. Everything about him overwhelms me—his size, his low voice. "I'll tell Mr. Scott my name."

In the shadowed space between us, his smile spreads, white and taunting. The pleasure that lights his strange yellow eyes is almost sensual, as if I caressed him. "You'll have to get past me."

My heart thuds. He likes that I'm challenging him, and God, that's even worse. What if I've already failed? I'm free-falling, tumbling, turning over without a single hope to anchor me. Where will I go if he turns me away? What will happen to my father?

"Let me go," I whisper, but my hope fades fast.

His eyes flash with warning. "Little Avery James, all grown up."

A small gasp resounds in the space between us. He already knows my name. That means he knows who my father is. He knows what he's done. Denials rush to my throat, pleas for understanding. The hard set of his eyes, the broad strength of his shoulders tells me I won't find any mercy here.

I square my shoulders. I'm desperate but not broken. "If you know my name, you know I have friends in high places. Connections. A history in this city. That has to be worth something. That's my collateral."

Those connections might not even take my call, but I have to try something. I don't know if it will be enough for a loan or even to get me through the door. Even so, a faint feeling of family pride rushes over my skin. Even if he turns me away, I'll hold my head high.

Golden eyes study me. Something about the way he said *little Avery James* felt familiar, but I've never seen this man. At least I don't think we've met. Something about the otherworldly glow of those eyes whispers to me, like a melody I've heard before.

On his driver's license it probably says something mundane, like brown. But that word can never encompass the way his eyes seem almost luminous, orbs of amber that hold the secrets of the universe. *Brown* can never describe the deep golden hue of them, the indelible opulence in his fierce gaze.

"Follow me," he says.

Relief courses through me, flooding numb limbs, waking me up enough that I wonder what I'm doing here. These aren't men, they're animals. They're predators, and I'm prey. Why would I willingly walk inside?

What other choice do I have?

I step over the veined marble threshold.

The man closes the door behind me, shutting out the rain and the traffic, the entire city disappeared in one soft turn of the lock. Without another word he walks down the hall, deeper into the shadows. I hurry to follow him, my chin held high, shoulders back, for all the world as if I were an invited guest. Is this how the gazelle feels when she runs over the plains, a study in grace, poised for her slaughter?

The entire world goes black behind the staircase, only breath, only bodies in the dark. Then he opens another thick wooden door, revealing a dimly lit room of cherrywood and cut crystal, of leather and smoke. Barely I see dark eyes, dark suits. Dark men.

I have the sudden urge to hide behind the man with the golden eyes. He's wide and tall, with hands that could wrap around my waist.

He's a giant of a man, rough-hewn and hard as stone.

Except he's not here to protect me.

He could be the most dangerous of all.

✧ ✧ ✧

The price of survival…
Gabriel Miller swept into my life like a storm. He tore down my father with cold retribution, leaving him penniless in a hospital bed. I quit my private all-girl's college to take care of the only family I have left.

There's one way to save our house, one thing I have left of value.

My virginity.

A forbidden auction…
Gabriel appears at every turn. He seems to take pleasure in watching me fall. Other times he's the only kindness in a brutal underworld.

Except he's playing a deeper game than I know. Every move brings us together, every secret rips us apart. And when the final piece is played, only one of us can be left standing.

"Skye Warren's THE PAWN is a triumph of intrigue, angst, and sensual drama. I was clenching everything. Gabriel and Avery

sucked me in from the first few paragraphs and never let go."

—New York Times bestselling author Annabel Joseph

Want to read more? The Pawn is available on Amazon, iBooks, Barnes & Noble, Kobo, and other book retailers!

Other Books by Skye Warren

Stripped series
Tough Love
Love the Way You Lie
Better When It Hurts
Even Better
Pretty When You Cry
Caught for Christmas
Hold You Against Me
To the Ends of the Earth

Chicago Underground series
Rough
Hard
Fierce
Wild
Dirty
Secret
Sweet
Deep

Criminals and Captives series
Prisoner

Standalone Dark Romance
Wanderlust
On the Way Home
His for Christmas
Hear Me
Take the Heat

Dark Nights series
Keep Me Safe
Trust in Me
Don't Let Go

The Beauty series
Beauty Touched the Beast
Beneath the Beauty
Broken Beauty
Beauty Becomes You
Beauty and the Beast (Boxed Set)
Loving the Beauty: A Beauty Epilogue

About the Author

Skye Warren is the New York Times bestselling author of contemporary romance such as the Chicago Underground and Stripped series. Her books have been featured in Jezebel, Buzzfeed, USA Today Happily Ever After, Glamour, and Elle Magazine. She makes her home in Texas with her loving family, two sweet dogs, and one evil cat.

Sign up for Skye's newsletter:
www.skyewarren.com/newsletter

Like Skye Warren on Facebook:
facebook.com/skyewarren

Join Skye Warren's Dark Room reader group:
skyewarren.com/darkroom

Follow Skye Warren on Instagram:
instagram.com/skyewarrenbooks

Visit Skye's website for her current booklist:
www.skyewarren.com

Copyright

This is a work of fiction. Any resemblance to actual persons, living or dead, business establishments, events or locales is entirely coincidental. All rights reserved. Except for use in a review, the reproduction or use of this work in any part is forbidden without the express written permission of the author.

To the Ends of the Earth © 2016 by Skye Warren
Print Edition

Cover design by Book Beautiful
Cover photograph by Sara Eirew
Formatting by BB eBooks

Made in the USA
Middletown, DE
21 March 2024